The Ballad of Billy N. M.

A Flash Opera

DSS Atkinson

Hearthside Stories

Contents

From a care home in London, England, Bill reminisces on life…

"Alright, mate, I'll let you go, my turn to call next week."

Indistinguishable chatter…

"Well yes, *really*, you just don't know when it's gonna happen, do ya? I mean, just the other night, a very, *very* old friend of mine came to visit, and I had to, rather awkwardly, pull him to one side and really sort of *say*, and sort of ask him, you know, 'I *thank* you, for err… for *coming* to my party. How are you and how was your drive over?' You know? Anyway, I'll call next time, I'll let you go."

Indistinguishable chatter…

"Well that's it. That's it, and I've mentioned before, being sat at the same restaurant, and that one fella who walked into the room, sort of, looked right at me, like he recognised me, and made a beeline for me… Well and I've said, I was thinking, is this fella gonna slow down? Or what's about to happen here? Right up to me he came, right up, and he put the plate down with our food on it and I had to stop him, didn't I? I did a quick double take at my order, and just really had to say, rather embarrassingly, 'err, excuse me, mate, I'm not a big fan of playing tennis'. I said, you know?"

Indistinguishable chatter…

"I'll let you go, mate, but I'll just say, I've always said that, always, you *give*, and you get back. You *give*, you get back. Always said that. Like… when the wife used to give me a short, sharp, *clip*… to the old… *manhood*, I'd always head straight outside, and the first fella I'd meet, I'd offer him one, you know? You give, you get back. *Always* said it."

Indistinguishable chatter…

"Well that's the problem, ain't it, not enough services about to get it fully solved. My own lad was telling me yesterday about the bins piling up, 'cause you know he works for the council, and he recons given enough time the bags will be stacked as high as houses. *High as houses*, he said. What we gonna do then, 'ey?"

Indistinguishable chatter…

"No, not got much down on paper lately, mate, the old writer's block, and my carer's say they don't want to leave me alone with the pens again… I prefer my last care home."

Indistinguishable chatter…

"I know, mate, I know. It's a right old oasis, I'll let you go, anyway."

Indistinguishable chatter…

"Alright, mate, I'll let you go. My turn to call next week."

…

Solution

Sorry about that... Where were we?

Right, I *suppose*, one of my first most *memorable* memories might've been... How should I put it? A day from my early youth, just a young'un, probably five or six. I was a skinny lad, little red head with a freckled face and blue eyes, not like now, bald and wrinkled now, can barely get about even with the walker, prefer to sit in my chair, it's a turner.

Anyway, I was playing in the back garden, only a little one it was. Grew up in a council house in the East End of London, suppose you could call me a Cockney, I ain't into all that silly slang nonsense though, not me, I talk *proper*, always have.

The house we lived in was a terraced, but like I said, it had a garden at least, somewhere me and my siblings would play. I was the youngest, and the only red head, and... well... I was the only one our dad didn't hit.

Somehow I'd managed to get my hands on a sort of *racket*, like a badminton or tennis handled thing, and what's a lad gonna do when he gets a hold of something like that?

I started hitting stones out of my mum and dad's back garden. Over the hedges. Was *whacking* them, hard as I could, suddenly heard a loud *CRACK* and a *SHATTER*. The feeling of panic that grabbed me then, blimey. I knew I'd done it, I hit the stone and I'd smashed something, but I was too scared to hang about and find out what.

I ran inside and hid up in my room. I was up there for about ten minutes I recon, but it felt like hours. I was sweating, I had a little cartoon bear painted on my blue wallpaper and I remember I kept looking at it, looking at its eyes, at its smile, it was so happy and I was so worried, I wanted to throw up.

After those ten minutes, just as I started to calm down, I heard my mum call my name. "Billy?" She said, softly.

"Yes, mummy?" I replied, staring at the bear on my wall.

"Can you come downstairs, please?"

"Why?" I asked, trying to sound innocent, like.

"Just come down, I need to ask you something." I took a moment, trying to make sure I wouldn't look suspicious, like I hadn't done anything wrong. I took a deep breath, and considered putting a hardback book down my pants in case I'd get a slap, but I thought that'd give me away anyway.

When I got downstairs the neighbours were in the living room. Three of them. Mum was stood there too, they were all lined up, all staring at me. I started to sulk a little bit but tried my best not to cry.

"Did you do it, Billy?" She asked. I couldn't imagine what trouble I was about to be in. Maybe I *would* get a slapped backside, maybe I'd be grounded, maybe I couldn't watch T.V. All my friends would know what I'd done, all my teachers, everyone at school, the whole world would know I'd smashed that glass.

"Do what, mummy?" I replied. My lower lip started trembling. I felt terrible.

She knelt in front of me with the fuming neighbours right by our side. "Billy, just be honest, you won't be in trouble with mummy. Did you do it?" She looked into my eyes, and the moment I answered, I had to look at the floor.

"No." I… I *lied*. "I didn't do it, mummy." That might be the worst thing I've ever said.

Mum had a big row with the neighbours that day, arguing I hadn't done it, 'cause I said I hadn't. I'd never seen her raise her voice like that, in my memories she'd always been quiet and timid, and later I'd know why… my dad drank a lot, he was always down the boozer, and when he'd get home… well… he'd be violent.

I don't know if mum believed me or not… Maybe she was more worried what the old man would do to her if she'd took the neighbour's side over mine. I lied to her, and 'cause of it I didn't get into trouble, the guilt though, it was worse than any good hiding could've been. Maybe she knew that… Who knows…

I never did own up, and it ate at me for years. Every time I saw those neighbours or walked past their house, I'd feel bad. I still think about it sometimes, even now… It's just one of those things you did as a child that you can't change, ain't it? We all must've done them…

I'll never forget that year, never, partly 'cause of what I'd done, but mostly 'cause there was some great stuff on T.V. around then.

My favourite programme was about a young lad who'd stumble upon strange and mysterious things. I used to watch it every morning. Every morning for years, without fail… About a smart lad, he spoke the Queen's English, like… Sometimes he was in the stories, sometimes he'd tell them. Great it was, every day I'd watch it, it was called… err… what was it called?

…

Well, I can't remember the name of it now…

Supersonic

"MAYDAY, MAYDAY, WE'VE HIT SOMETHING!"

"*WAKE UP, CAPTAIN!*"

"ARE YOU OKAY, CAPTAIN?"

I had never felt better. My limbs were all stretched out, somehow, like I was being crucified. There was no pain, in fact, it was the opposite of pain. I felt *numb,* mentally and physically *pinned* by some massive G-force, *but… against what?*

"Captain, can you hear us?"

"Of course I hear you," I muttered, disinterested in the drama. "What's all the screaming about?"

"Captain, we've taken on an emergency course down to Earth's surface… We will need to eject in the escape pod to survive, our descent speeds are growing rapidly." Ah, it was flooding back to me now. Space station. Cosmonaut. *I'm a Cosmonaut.*

I could see through a window, we certainly were falling rapidly, that halo of deadly radiation skimming off our magnetosphere was fully visible.

"No problem," I said, but now I thought about it, I couldn't remember how we'd gotten into this situation. I stared out at the view of Earth. It captured me. From frozen tundras, to deserts, jungles and oceans, *every* beautiful detail was visible, I could see every last ingredient of *life*. "Out of curiosity…" I mumbled… sheepishly. "What's happened?"

"Sir, we think you were knocked unconscious when we hit the passing spud, there was radio silence, and no physical responses… Sir… you're… not inside the station… You're hooked to it by a tether." The very notion was confusing. "Our ship will hit the upper echelons of our atmosphere soon… We need to eject before we burst into flames… and die." The line fell quiet, unsurprisingly.

They weren't joking. I noticed now, I weren't looking out of a window, it was my spacesuit's protective head visor. I felt dizzy. "Do what you need to." I think I said. My body's pressure pinned against the station's exterior felt unbearable, and as the arch of our stunning world's upper atmosphere ceased to reflect the sun's rays, I had a burning idea that *needed* to be seen through.

I *needed* to look at my station one last time. *Needed to.* That vessel I'd spent the best days of my life on. I bucked my body, thrusted my legs and pushed back with everything I had, twisting my hips with a howl of pain for the feeling of my suit and craft combusting in the ozone. *One last time*, I saw what carried me through our world's skies.

It was a yellow submarine, and it made me laugh.

Gums

I walked into the waterside hanger, and there they were. Two, twenty something foot, *hulking* great white sharks, hoisted from the water by their tails and strung up.

One of them was limp. Its gigantic gills hung open exposing deep red tissues beneath thick, sandpaper like skin.

The other writhed, arching its back, biting fist sized razors at the air in a frenzy. I couldn't believe my eyes. There was a crowd around the hanger's water tank, many of them gazing down into the unstirring wash.

"WHAT'S GOING ON?" I yelled, shocked and appalled at the sight. From the water ahead of me an explosion gushed upwards into the air, and through the rush of foam a body was slung.

Beyond, deep in the water, I saw the glinting white sheen of an enormous beast.

The human screamed out as they splashed back into the tank, laughing and hollering in their fall. "Again!" They yelled to a nearby guard. "I want to go again!"

"Get out of the water!" The figure called back. "You'll have to pay again if you want to go again." The guard paced over to me and grabbed my arm. "What are you doing here, do you know Windsor?" I shook my head.

"No, I... What's going on? Why are these sharks strung up? What's in the water?" The guard looked back at the pool, then at the sharks hanging from the rafters, then at me.

"Shark attacks."

"*Shark attacks?*" All I could do was repeat him. "*What?*"

"Windsor completely removes their teeth, *all* of them. Then we let them attack. Nobody gets hurt, spare a few broken ribs here and there." He pointed back towards the strung up apex predators. "They die quickly in captivity, though, so we try to have a few spare." The enormous lines of horrific jaws looming in the background both began thrashing about.

"*Why?*" I asked.

The guard shrugged.

Shufflers

"*Mommy?* Can we dress up this year?" Little Freddie asked, playing in the corner with his toys. He was facing the wall, and had been all evening. He wanted to turn and look at his mommy, but was worried. She'd been shuffling in and out of the room all day, and had not once called his name, not since her shadow changed.

Mommy's and Daddy's shadows never looked like that. Not until today.

"Mommy?" Freddie asked again. He heard his mommy's shuffling stop. Silence took the room. Freddie watched the wall, nervously, the shadow did not move, nor did he hear his mommy's call. With welling tear ducts, little Freddie looked back down at his toys, holding on tight to his Jack-o-Lantern.

Amping

He did good horror stories, that lad, or whoever wrote those episodes, sometimes I'd imagine myself in the scenarios. Those horrors were always my favourite, and of course, they inspired me to write my own, I was obsessed with them, ever since I was a young'un.

It made me want to be a screenwriter, a famous one if I could, funny what you see when you're a kid, and what sticks with you, ain't it? Just watching a T.V programme as a little lad got me obsessed with it for the rest of my life. *Mad* really, what ideas we have as young'uns.

I really did make a go for it as well, used to love writing fiction, and screenplays, poems for the missus, the whole lot. '*Between the Mares*' was what I called my collection, 'cause I'd have vivid dreams all the time, you see, and when I was a youngster, I thought they were scary, nightmares, you know? As I got older, I really quite enjoyed them, and when I'd wake up I'd write them down… that's where all my ideas came from, from the 'mares' I'd have… *that*, and there were some I sort of… well… *nicked.*

I aimed to make a huge collection, create a masterpiece, but somewhere along the line I recon I stopped dreaming. I don't really remember them at all these days, in fact… sometimes… there's things I don't think I remember all together… but maybe I never knew them in the first place.

Anyway, if we get time today, I'll show you some, if you like?

In fact… here you go, look, this is one I first came across when I was at school, one I put my own spin on. Don't remember how old, but I still got it, like to keep it close to me these days, just to remind me about how things used to be, back when I was a bit more dexterous in the brains department.

It's a well known one, sort of... *stole* the idea... in a manner of speaking... you might already be familiar with it...

The Guitar Man

In the beginning, Earth was formless and empty, just a scorching red orb spinning in the vastness of the universe to a single discordant hum. In its tempered state the core began to cool, calmly, softly, the surface slowly solidified and lighter elements separated, their faintest frictions fracturing the peace.

Protons and electrons collided in a race to settle amidst their natural orders. Through the churning turbulence precipitation gathered across Earth's skies, the tempests bulged and swirled, twisting until their contents could be contained no more.

Lightning split the horizon, clouds burst and poured, hammering against Earth's dry, barren surface, drumming melodies and sounds into the atmosphere. With the hailing rains, a grand orchestra began, new rhythms arose and oceans swelled, their surfaces pounded through the rousing weathers, rippling a potent resonance through the sea.

The unrelenting frequencies arranged and re-arranged micro-nutrients and minerals for untold eons, unthinkable numbers of formations and failures, vibrating, splitting and regurgitating, billions of cycles until a reverberating assembly secured themselves.

Simple cells united, filtering, feeding, resting and sleeping, brightening the oceans and swirling new sounds beneath Earth's calming waves. She was whole, and radiated with a unique magnificence.

Each new development of matter caused another shudder to stir through Earth's beautiful forms, the excitement invigorating competition, more complex collections emerged from the turmoil and the first predators spawned between plants and plankton, the first vertebrates appeared, carnivores and omnivores and the great orchestra became louder, the collisions far vaster and harmonies much faster.

The bubbling oceans crowded, struggling to harbour their ever-growing populations. Earth's inhabitants grew weary, fearful, their faeces turning her waters green with pollution, and those struggling to survive took sights to her tranquil lands.

As before, experiments unfolded, untold failures were witnessed, unheard of sounds made as seabound life crawled ashore, pushing onto beaches and swimming up rivers, embedding themselves into Earth's lush undergrowth, dragging their pestilence with them.

Her body was breached, its sides giving way to an overflow of organic oddities, churning and forcing the slimy bog from which they wretched across the continent. From the murky, oily swamps, a bipedal figure of skin and bone arose, slouched and timid, struggling to claw its limbs clear of the vibrating detritus.

It led the race, and in its wake, pollution and corruption followed. The waste covered entity twitched and convulsed in its adolescence, struggling to make sense of its surroundings, being allured and drawn in towards a vibrant, blazing singularity.

Something was already present…

The Guitar Man drew fingers across his frets. With inconceivable rapidity he played, each new key and octane he broke or rose into saw the oceans mix and lands tremble, saw the gruesome shapes swimming amidst their filth consume one another in a frenzied gluttony.

Life swarmed to him. Micro-organisms flocked in their trillions, insects and birds, lizards and mammals, drawn with fascinating intrigue to the charming melody rippling through Earth's skies, each plucked note causing colourful auroras to ride the ionosphere, encircling and encasing it, enticing all.

Nature poured from the primordial quagmires, gathering round, still fighting and struggling amongst themselves to cast gaze upon the piper. Faster and faster he picked, his sounds resonating through jungles and forests, fish leapt from the waters, bugs metamorphosed, bipeds lit fires and alligators rolled. Horses bucked and lions roared, ecstasy pulsed as existence came together.

Every last miniscule cell made its way along the waterways to reach the strumming entity, licking and riffing, never residing, never letting up until all that had come into being arrived, hypnotised, they gazed involuntarily at the glowing source, *a vision of perfection.*

He clasped down on his strings. Feedback ripped through his amplifier. His bass shredded into infinity blasting a shockwave through the masses, the last chord followed by a haunting echo. Wailing screams of extinction howled across Earth's surface, its note turning all to dust.

The vibrations faded. The rivers of plague resided, spreading rot ceased where life had dragged it. The Guitar Man released his grip and waited for silence…

…Absolute…

…Silence…

Peering out, with a toothless grin, empty eye sockets gauged the reading of his next masterpiece.

Ingrained

First time I saw that concept, I thought... I wonder if I'll ever have any ideas as good as that... It's a real shame I can't strictly call it my own... But *anyway*, I was saying all this started when I was a young'un.

My school years weren't all that eventful if I'm honest, well, not inside school, outside was always a case of tiptoeing around at home, 'cause like I said, my dad was a wrong'un, and there were a bunch of us crammed in our little house, even a creaking floorboard would gather unwanted attention when he was about... Those were honestly some years I could do with forgetting.

Sometimes school weren't much better. I remember this one teacher, I can't even remember his name, who now I think back about, well I can really say he was a wrong'un as well.

I had more slippers across the backside from him than I can count. "Six of the best!" He would shout... *Six of the best...* He would bend you over in the school yard and give you a good whacking, no one would stop him, none of the other teachers, they'd just turn a blind eye to it. Humiliating it was. I wouldn't get hit at home, but I certainly did at school. I'm sure I weren't a bad lad, but he would always go for me. *Six of the best...* I dunno...

I had a thing for this one girl, beautiful blonde she was, but I was too shy to talk to her, even though she said she had a thing for me back, just too shy I was... probably the most beautiful *thing* I ever saw. That same teacher once made me shower naked in front of the whole class, he watched, too, and she was there to see it.

I couldn't look her in the face afterwards, couldn't look no one in the face after that.

I dunno why he did it, but after I got out, he rushed over and grabbed me, said I hadn't washed my hair, called me a 'dirty little boy'. He turned the shower on cold and held me under there until I cried. Grown fella holding a young lad naked under the water until he cried.

Hard to forget things like that, and strange to think about why a grown man would be stood about watching a young'un having a shower, you know? I suppose at the time you don't put much thought to it, but some things make more sense when you've got a few years under your belt.

Of course, as you'd expect, things did catch up with him. When we'd all grown up, it showed on the news one day, had his name up on the screen, and a picture, it was him, orange jumpsuit, mug shot and all. He'd been arrested after all those years, things finally caught up.

Said he was sent down for throwing a pineapple at a copper's head.

Rainbow

On the day I turned 16 I found out my dad died. I hadn't seen or spoken to him for five years. The last time I saw him he broke my mum's cheekbone. That was when we left. He never hit me, but he hit my older siblings like he'd hit my mum. He drank a lot, and when he was drunk... that's when he was the worst.

We never owned the house he died in, it was the one I grew up in though, the council were going to take it back and contacted my mum to see if she would help clear it, in case there was anything there that might be of any value. I don't think she wanted to, still, she'd always been kind-hearted and a bit of a pushover, so she said yes.

She asked if I'd come with her, and of course, I did.

It was a mess inside. It smelt of mould. The walls were stained yellow and the floorboards were all grubby. There were empty bottles and dirty cutlery everywhere. It never looked like that before, mum kept everything clean and tidy.

The front door caught the wind on our way in and SLAMMED hard. Mum flinch. "Sorry, mum." I said, feeling the slam myself. *That sound.* I remembered that door slamming and knew what it meant. It was sad to see her still react like that, even though she knew he was gone.

"Where should we start?" I asked, trying to move her attention. She opened the under stairs cupboard and looked inside.

"There's some boxes in here," mum said, "shall we get them into the living room and start there?"

"Yeah, sure." I took a bunch out and cleared some rubbish off the dining table, noticing an old line engraved on one of its wooden legs. I pointed to it. "Remember when Geoff fell off his chair at dinner?" Mum laughed.

My oldest brother lived down south now. He weren't interested in coming back. None of them were.

The boxes were mostly full of old bills and legal papers. One of the smaller ones had a bunch of pictures in it though. There were lots of people I didn't recognise, but plenty I did. The first one I saw of mum she was sat with her sister in an old pub.

"Remember that, mum?" I showed her it and she smiled.

"That was auntie Kat's birthday." She said, moving round the table to join me.

"How old were you?" It was funny seeing old photos of my family, they always looked so... *weird*.

"Oh, I don't know, early twenties?" She laughed a little again and took out another photo. It was mum's and dad's wedding day. All the family was there. Everyone looked so happy, especially mum. She looked at it for a moment then put it down. "Lots of old faces." She said, retaking the one of her sister.

"When did you last see auntie Kat?" I asked, picking another picture from the bunch. Mum sighed quietly.

"Not for years." I'm not sure why I asked. I suddenly felt stupid. I knew why she hadn't seen any of her friends or family for so long.

"Is *that* you?" There was a black and white photo with a group of young women posing in ballerina outfits. Mum took it and her face lit up.

"That's my old dance group." She said.

"*What?*" I was shocked. "I never knew you used to dance." She nodded, looking over the image.

"Before you were born!" This time I laughed.

"Were you any good?"

"We were alright." Her posture in the image looked so confident. Such a huge contrast to how I'd see her stood around my dad, and even now, years after she'd gotten away from him. "Our teacher had us listed for auditions in London to try out for a big live stage performance. It was my dream once, to get up in the lights, ever since I was a little girl."

"Did you go?" Her smile faded. She shook her head. "How come?" I asked. Mum looked at the wedding photo again.

"I met your father... He was different then, and life... gets in the way. He persuaded me to move with him for work, then we had kids, we had you," she smiled again, "and bills to pay... and arguments..."

"Sorry, mum," I mumbled, "stupid of me to ask."

"It's alright, sweetie," she said, looking back at her dance group with a distance stare. "*They were only dreams.*"

Pandemic

I was a teenager when I first heard whispers of it, only 17, as I walked through my store's warehouse on my first day at work.

"*So-and-So* won't be in tonight," the area manager said to a colleague who I never got a chance to know. "Think you could cover his shift?"

"Sure," he replied, "what's wrong with him?" I heard him ask.

"He said his doctor called it... *Something...* 'Blindness'... Keep it to yourself, though."

"Wait, *what?* He's blind?" The worker sounded shocked.

"I'm not sure, he said there's no symptoms... he just said 'blindness'... *Something*, blindness, again, I don't want to cause a stir, so keep it to yourself." He nodded to our manager, and that was the last I thought I'd ever hear of it.

As my days at work passed me by, the weeks turned to months, the individual who fell ill returned and as far as I know, when questioned on his ailments, he had no answers, he just couldn't make it in that day due to the 'blindness'.

Every now and then you'd hear of another name ringing in, not turning up for their shift, and when they returned, they could never quite explain the symptoms. "*It was the blindness... I... I just couldn't make it.*"

The problem reached the news one day, I remember hearing it on the radio, the same year I got my promotion to area manager. It seemed it wasn't just an isolated case to my store, all across the country, numerous people were struggling to turn up to work.

They just… couldn't make it. "It's the blindness." They'd say… *the blindness.*

By my fifth year I'd reached senior management. The store was struggling, and so was the nation. More than half the workforce was just… *gone…* and it was all over the news every day. T.V, newspapers, internet, radio, you name it, this mysterious *blindness* was preventing people from coming to work. Most no longer rang in ill, they just stopped turning up.

My mind was constantly on the subject, troubled thoughts for my ill colleagues and for the struggling workplaces up and down the country. *What's happening?* I asked, over and over, each day I drove to work, when I got home and ate dinner with my family, when I kissed my wife goodnight. *What is this incurable disease, and what if it gets me?*

Well… one day I woke up. The house was empty. The kids were at school. The wife out shopping. It was an important day. A meeting of CEO's, one my director had invited me to, to forward my career, but I knew the very moment I awoke in that empty house… I'd been afflicted.

I noticed myself breathing. *I never thought about breathing.* I reached for the bedside table and picked up my phone. With a shaking hand, and a shameful embarrassment, I dialled my boss' number. It rang, and rang, and rang… until…

"Sir? It's Maxwell."

"Ah, Maxwell! Looking forward to the meeting?"

"Sir… I won't be making it in this morning, I… I think I've got it."

"What? Maxwell? No, what's wrong?"

"Sir, I… I can't quite explain it."

"What do you mean, Maxwell? Is it the blindness?"

I nodded to nobody. "I think so, sir… I think It's the blindness." That very rare sound of an empty house was so, *so* blissful.

"Maxwell, nobody ever has *any* answers, please tell me, what's wrong with you? There must be *some* symptoms, ANYTHING!" He yelled down the phone at me. I was laying on my back. I couldn't move, I JUST. COULD. NOT. GET. UP.

"*Sir?*"

"*Maxwell?*"

"Sir, I think…" I looked across the bed. My lower lip trembled. I felt a wheeziness surge up within me and I began to blubber. "I… I think it's… *anal…* sir."

"*WHAT?*" He yelled again. He sounded furious. "*Anal Blindness?*" With tears in my eyes I nodded again to myself.

"Anal Blindness, sir."

"What do you mean, Maxwell? WHAT IS IT? WHY CAN'T YOU MAKE IT?"

"Sir…" I glanced with blurred sight down at my duvet covered body. The house was so peaceful, *I never got this…* I was warm and comfortable, there was no stress here, no responsibility, no… *work.* "I *just…* can't…"

"Can't what, Maxwell? PLEASE, what is this 'Anal Blindness'? Just tell me!" I took a deep breath, and ended the call before speaking aloud.

"I just can't see my arse… getting out of bed this morning."

Warehouse

Amidst an open top keep, its walls demolished and still smouldering, burnt black and ruined, whatever woodwork once helped its foundations hold were no more, a baker's dozen of ragged nobles stood with emergency around half a charcoal table.

"The army is *gone*. Burned to *death* whilst the others flee for their lives. They will not return to Kingdom until this *thing* is gone." Panicked mumbles filled what was left of the hall. The tapestry once lining its pristine brickwork had been reduced to ashes.

"There are no more who dare chase such things!" As the very sentence fell to a still, a pounding clap and thud burst the keep's doors wide open. Its inhabitants flinched, turning to look at the entrance with horror strewn across them.

The skies above drew tight and grey. Dark, dark clouds, holding their water with a fervent greed, they looked heavy as though to drop the entire sky with their weight.

At the end of the keep's tunnel, in the fading light, a champion burned with glistening armour. Every step he took forward he appeared to grow, until he filled the entirety of the doorway where the nobles stood.

"*I HAVE HEARD OF YOUR TROUBLES, MAGGOTS, I VENTURE BACK FROM VICTORY TO SECURE YOUR RATDOM.*" The nobles mumbled amongst themselves. Some sounded angry. Most were submissive. There was nothing they could dispute.

"Please, white knight, can you save us?"

*"WHITE KNIGHT? YOU KNOW ME ALL MY
LIFE AND YOU REFER TO ME AS, WHITE
KNIGHT?"*

"Arthur!" One yelled out, reluctantly. "Arthur,
we know it is only you who can perform this task,
please, we offer anything."

"AND ANYTHING I WILL TAKE." With
confusion, the men looked about. One went to speak.
Another held up his hand, forefinger raised.

"Take what you will." They whimpered at their
overbearing imprisoner. "Just say the price, and take
what you will."

Satisfied, the named NPC rode out beyond the
walls of his noble's keep. The weather did not let up as
he crossed country far and wide. Through trees and
fields, along valleys and up endless mountain passes,
until AT LAST, the unstoppable force reigned his
beautiful horse back upon a precipice, preventing her
from falling a hundred miles down.

A white streak of lightening ripped through
eternity, exploding against the arch of the glass wall.

There stood the Dragon.

With a mighty call of heroism, Arthur charged at
the fearsome terror, holding his lance poised with
steadfast determination. Rainwater battered off his metal
plate, falling into the earth beneath, fading into silence.
This is it. The butcher would be gone, *at last.*

His horse thundered on with a ferocious gait,
snorting with confidence, it's rider bellowing orders of
execution through his impenetrable aegis, and as he
enclosed upon the gigantic lizard's beating chest, he was
crushed beneath its enormous claw. Stomped and

squashed effortlessly, his blood and bones, and those limbs of his horse's splattered everywhere, staining the stone with a hot streak of lifeless sinewy matter.

His lance had loosed, though, it travelled true, embedding itself into the beast's pumping heart.

"*Arthur Job, well done.*" He wheezed his last essence of life away, and faded into the grey of immemorabilia, that given enough time, no one would really care about.

Crossroad

They were a mad rollercoaster, those retail years, working in the warehouse, trying to impress the bosses, thinking I was better than them, thinking I could do it without them, thinking anyone cared if I worked fifty hours a week overtime to fix the company's problems, thinking they *needed* me, actually turning up when most of the work force was pulling sickies and not giving a damn.

Nobody cared, of course, you could put your everything into it, fail the task, get sacked or quit, and the next day they'd have some other would be hero in your place, like you'd never existed.

I hated every second of it. Don't miss them, never missed them, only half good thing that came of them was I met my first wife, lovely little brunette, or, well, I thought she was anyway… there were a few things she was deceptive about, let me tell you… but I'll say, I'm not one for moaning, not that I remember…

I'll put it like this… Within about six months of quitting my job, and it was a decent payer by the time I knocked it on the head, she filed for divorce, took the house off me, got full custody of our kids and blocked me from seeing them. That hurt. She took most of what money I'd managed to save up, took my *hair*, went bald I did, probably the bloody stress, and you know what really got me upset the most? Of all the things that happened during those six months?

It was only *then* she revealed she was a red head. *That's* when I found out, right at the end, she'd been lying all this time, had me thinking she was a brunette!

We had a lot of shared friends, and when it all went down, every single one of them sided with her.

The amount of things I heard I'd *said* or *done* that simply weren't true… well… needless to say, it got me pretty down, I mean, even after she revealed she was a red head, after claiming she was a brunette *all* them years people *still* sided with her… I don't know, like I say though, I'm not one for moaning… maybe it was 'cause I lied to my mum all that time ago… who knows.

Anyway! That was that, I was twenty five, had been married, divorced, had two kids I couldn't see no more, who I'd be paying towards for the next fifteen odd years, I was *bald*, had no job, no house to live in… Tell you what, I was down on my luck… down and *out.*

Only thing I had that kept me attached to life was a little black book with some nightmares written inside.

Half

"Another please, bartender!" I've started going out alone. Haven't had a missus for years. No mates around these days either, those that weren't shared with the ex are all off doing their own thing. Moving town, moving country, pretty successful as well, not like me, not now. "And make it sharpish!"

Had the same job for years. *Years*. Bleeding warehouse. Night shifts for years, now I ain't even got that. Just dole money, or the rock'n'roll as I prefer to call it, so sod it, may as well just get drunk.

I see old boys in here most of the time. Old timers. Probably lonely, probably fought in the war, all their kids moved away, wives died. Now they just go to the pub to kill the day, killing those last few days of what misery is left in their lonely lives. One at a time, one hour, one minute. It's *pathetic*.

I'll have another piss whilst Baz pours my pint, I got a tab anyway, and it ain't like these stools are filling up, not on a Tuesday night. Once the canal opens up that's it, every five minutes, straight to the pisser. Can't see straight, can still find my member though, but don't matter how many times I shake it, *I still get a dribble*. Don't understand it. Just… *always* get a dribble.

Washing my hands and looking in the mirror again. At least I wash my hands, see a lot of them don't even bother with that. Don't much like the look of what's in the mirror. Barely gone thirty and I'm bald. Got wrinkle lines on my forehead, frown lines they call them. Damn right I've been frowning. What's there to live for. I'm pathetic and I got nothing. Not now, only this next pint. Off I go.

Seems there's a beauty just come in. Nice legs. She's sat where I was sat, got a little cup where I had my pint, and the pint pourers just put my new pint next to her and looked at me. Now I got a sweat on, what was I thinking about again?

"Sorry, mind if I just grab that glass?" I say to her, reaching over, hoping she doesn't notice the streams accumulating at my temples.

"Go ahead," she says back, smiling, nice smile, bet she thinks I look a right mug. Alone at a bar, bald and full of frown lines.

"Thanks, sorry to disturb you." I try to pull the glass away.

"No worries, here often?" She asks, I can feel a warm rush coming on. Weren't expecting an attractive bird to start talking to me, at least Baz the barman's out of earshot.

"Not really, not local, just passing through and thought I'd grab a quick pint." Good old bollocks saves the day. "You?" Like she's going to be interested in chatting to a mug like me...

...

Well... I can't keep that nonsense up, talking like that, but that's really how I was for a while, really how I was behaving, for a long while in fact. Always *drunk*, and thinking like *that*. I just couldn't pull myself clear of the self-loathing, and lack of self-belief, until that night, that is, when I met her, just by sheer chance.

For some reason she wanted to chat, started talking to me like I'd known her for years. Ever meet those kinds of people? Rare it is, to meet someone you just click with straight away. All sorts we were nattering about, land sites up and down the country, T.V programmes, I told her about the mysteries I'd watch, she'd seen a few of them too.

We got another couple of drinks in and sat chatting some more, must've been a couple of hours we spoke, up until she did a double take at her watch and announced she had to shoot off.

"Alright, lovely to meet you," I said, the sweats had stopped by then, probably looked half smooth! "Think I can take your number? Would love to talk again, you're really lovely." I said, cornily.

"Oh, I'm so sorry," she replied, "I should've mentioned, I was waiting to catch the train across the road to go and meet my boyfriend."

"Oh," I said back, "oh, yeah no problem, my mistake." We'd been speaking hours and she'd never mentioned it. We were getting on so well I thought, but she never mentioned it. I felt like a numpty… an absolute *mug*, why should I've assumed she was single though?

She weren't miserable like me, how I was back then, I should've known. She was just passing through and being friendly. I went back to the toilet and looked in the mirror again, starring at my bald head, at my frown lines. *God* I was empty.

Well… I went back to the bar, but that particular evening weren't just another one wasted, and although I think back to asking that girl for her number and still cringe to this day, the night sticks in my head for other reasons.

I did some serious thinking over my last pint, some *serious* thinking, and I must admit, some truly bleak things crossed my mind, but no matter how dark those thoughts got, everything kept going back to my little black book, to my childhood nightmares.

I thought about them all the time, always had, all throughout school, throughout those years in the warehouse, getting churned out in that damned place. I decided what I was going to do, I was gonna get my nightmares out of the pages, and get after it.

It was time to start writing screenplays, properly, not just scribbling half-finished ideas down here and there, but really seeing them through to the finish, and to get them sent to whoever I could.

What could go wrong? I recon I saw the very bottom of the barrel that night, and I had nothing to lose.

Lidders

I don't remember how old I was when I saw those eyes reflecting in the headlights. I could see the outlines of the animals, too. They were deer. Lots of them. All stood stiff, staring at us through the night. Then an enormous metal door closed over my view, and the vehicle I was in started going down, *down* in some big elevator, more than big enough for just us.

I don't ever remember going back up that elevator. When it touched down I met a lot of people, most young like me. They would make us sit in classes, those who took us down there, that is.

In class they would say we were *special*… That we could see… *dangerous things* behind the darks of our eyelids, and we were important because of it. None of us had ever seen a thing though, or at least, I know I never had.

Sometimes we would play football in a large hall, and I'm sure I can remember, at one time, somebody got married. It was so bright that day, and green… but… I don't ever remember going *back up*.

When we slept, we all slept together. A hundred or more of us, all cramped up in the same place we played football. The floors were cold and hard. They said it was for *us*, for our own safety.

They would lock the doors, close us inside and turn out the lights. It was always calm then, when it was dark, so calm, and I would see nothing. It would feel like… like some *waters* were still. I enjoy water, too.

We have a heated swimming pool I use often. We have to go in groups of ten. Today I was the last one leaving… and I've had an accident… the back of my head hurts and I think I might be bleeding.

When my eyes were closed I thought my friends saw me slip. I thought they were running to help me… *such strange bodies…* My eyes are open now. It wasn't my friends rushing to me, they've all gone and…

I… I think they're here.

I don't want to blink again. Every time I blink they get closer, and move so *strangely… so, so strangely*. My eyes feel dry and heavy, they're itching but I…

Oh no.

Results

Took me three years of sending out scripts and getting rejected until I finally caught someone's eye, funny it should've been a little horror about *eyes* that done the job, 'ey?

I'd been single and lonely for *years* by then. Bald, single, and lonely. Still living in a one room council flat, taking up space, giving nothing back to society. It weren't until I finally pulled my thumb out I started being worth something, something I can look back at now and think, well, think I can at least give a nod of acknowledgement to, 'cause before then, I really was a waste of skin, needed a good shaking I did.

The chance meeting with that girl got me thinking, got me *moving*, just a chance meeting, and *well*… I have no idea who she was, but I couldn't thank her enough for the chat we had. Never saw her again, neither, like some kind of fairy, or guardian angel in the night. She swooped in to save me at my darkest hour… Whoever she was, I really am thankful to her.

Strangely, the only real positive thing I can say I took from those years was knowing, and really becoming familiar with the feeling of complete and utter *lowness*, if it's even a word. Depression, the very bottom, and that's because, for all those years I'd spent in that sorry state, having my work turned away just didn't have no effect on me.

My spirit couldn't be killed any more. I *had* no spirit. Nothing. So I never really thought much of the rejections when I started sending my screenplays out.

I couldn't be disappointed with anything more than I was at myself, so having another good-as anonymous stranger tell me they weren't interested in what I had to offer was like water off a gnat's chuff, so to speak.

The fella who *finally* picked me up, I'd later come to know, was of some half-respectable significance in the T.V and showbiz industry. First time I met him was quite the memorable event, too, *quite* the memorable event!

Shortly after he offered me his services, he invited me out to L.A. He lived in a flat, and it weren't a big place, not much bigger than mine if I'm honest, but I tell you what, it was expensive there, and the interior was like a rainbow. Everywhere you looked, bright, flashy artwork, big fur rugs and coloured leather sofas, it was the opposite of my dark grey hovel in London.

We spoke for some time about my work, and my dreams, my long-term dreams that is, and also what I'd been up to, up until that point in my life. Well, what could I really say that wouldn't bring the mood down?

I missed out most of the bleak stuff, didn't see much use in telling him what a loser I was. Whilst we sat and spoke, we both drank what he told me was a cup of tea... but my goodness, whatever was in the drink, and it did taste like tea, can't have been...

You ever seen a cat, a lion, and a stegosaurus in a back yard? At night it happened, if memory serves... though it rarely does these days...

Weren't long after finishing my drink, my agent mentioned his cat hadn't come back in for its supper, so I headed to the back door. A little wall lamp was on out there, pretty dim, but it let me see some distance, anyhow, I started calling his cat. "Pspspsps", you know

the noise you make to get a cat's attention? "Pspspsps."
Like that.

I heard the foliage in the dark EXPLODE and I
stumbled back thinking I'm gonna have a heart attack! I
turned for the backdoor and heard these *heavy* pads. Just
as I scrambled inside and shut the door some massive
figure *slammed* into the thing, on the outside!

I could see through the door, and I tell you, it was
a damned mountain lion, and it was *fierce*, hissing,
spitting, clawing. My heart was pounding, my skin was
crawling. "*Danny!*" I heard my agent shout, louder than
a foghorn! "We got us a lion in the yard!" Dunno where
this fella came from, didn't even know anyone else was
there. He was huge, and comes running through the
living room and grabs a rifle from above the hearth. I
remember the embers still scorching away beneath.

This *Danny* fella rushed over and aimed his gun
through the door at the lion, yelling all kinds of curse
words. It hissed at us all, big loud *HISS!* And it spat and
growled then doubled back on itself.

"Let's go after it!" Danny shouted, clutching his
gun tight.

"Are you mad?" I yelled back.

"He's right." My agent said.

"No he bloody isn't!" I said.

"We got too much live-stock in the yard to be
letting that animal think it can walk round our farm!" My
eyes widened bigger than fifty pence pieces I recon. The
mad lad pulled open the door and let loose two rounds
into the air. I didn't hear them go off, but I saw them.

"C'mon, we better go check on the hens." Danny
said, and together we crept outside. We were quiet, I was
scared. We traced around the lawn towards a barn, way

41

out in the dark it was, and then stopped to look up at a stegosaurus.

It was a huge, beautiful animal. Those dermal plates were something fierce, and those tusk things on its tail. It was so massive you could see it leering out from the side of the building. Its head looked a bit odd, looked like the eyeballs were missing, which was very strange to me.

So anyway, we got to the chicken coop, and we're checking our 360 ALL the time, because we're still freaked out about this damned lion attack. "What's that?" Danny asked, and I looked at him, and he was looking at my agent who was looking up. So we all looked up.

There was the cat, in the *air!* Right amongst the trees it was, with the whitest light you've ever seen coming out of its mouth, like it had swallowed a 6000lumen LED… or something. Light was literally exploding from its mouth! And it was blowing around, *backwards*, through the air like when you blow a balloon up and don't tie it, but just let go.

"Should I shoot her down?" The Danny fella asked, aiming his gun.

"*No!*" My agent screamed. Well, if I was scared before, *then* I was terrified. "You can't just shoot her!" He shouted again. "Let's get back inside! Something's not right." *Something's not right* he said, can you believe it? He weren't sure what, but he knew *something* weren't. Danny had already started running, he weren't hanging about. We sprinted after him, got inside, and locked the door behind us.

Next thing I know the cat-flap *slammed* hard as anything! I leapt out of my wits! Heavy breathing and panicking, only to realise I was *now* laying against my agent's sofa, on the floor, leaning on the side of it. It was daylight outside and my head was spinning a hundred miles an hour…

I could remember sitting, chatting to him, in his living area on the sofa, just chatting away, next thing I knew, this… *Big Dan* fella was wielding a bloody gun! Only thing was, come morning, I was looking around the flat and there weren't nobody else there, weren't no gun, and there certainly weren't no back door or yard to walk out in to. I could hear the cars streaming past outside, down on the high street. We were in a block of high-rising flats…

Around the room I could see a lion-fur rug, a half built papier-mache sort of dinosaur thing, and a stuffed cat on the mantlepiece… and I could only stand there and wonder what on *Earth* had happened.

When my agent finally appeared he started laughing, near to tears he got with his chuckling, "Did ya have a good night?" He asked with that American twang. That's all he said, and then I started laughing too. We laughed and laughed, couldn't stop!

He had to leave early that morning, and I was due back in England. He told me I should only have one aim in my life once I got home. To produce the best horror scripts I could come up with, and he would do the rest.

I can't tell you what happened the night before, but I can tell you, as I stood in his flat, head spinning like nothing, in that moment, I knew *it* was happening. They wanted my scripts, so out came my little black book, and I went to work…

Scouters

Huddled nervously around the embers of a dying fire, in the depths of a pitch black night, a group of minors sat listening with deep intrigue to their scout leader. Their eyes were fixated on his face and the torchlight he cast across it, causing his features to dip and meld with the fluctuating flames *spitting* away.

"Beware the black-eyed children, they look innocent, just like you, they will pretend to be your friends! They creep through the woodlands at night, sometimes on all fours, scraping on tents and doors, looking for their mothers, asking to be let in... But you should NEVER let them in." The children jumped at their scout leader's dramatics.

That'll get the little shits. Tony thought to himself, watching with delight whilst the horror grew across them. They'd been lazy all day, *probably the older group telling them I've got no real authority here.* They might not be in the military now, but he knew of other ways to shock them into shape.

"Right, Cannock Chase scout troop! Off to your marquees, and *NO* lights. I want *silence*. Get some sleep, we've got a long way to go in the morning."

"Do we have to go already, sir?" One of the lads asked, raising an arm.

"What about the children from the story? I don't want to camp out now." He heard a few of the youngest scouts whimpering amongst themselves, and it brought him a strangely sadistic glee. *Pussies.*

"We're out here for the night and that's that! If you want to walk the 30 miles back to basecamp on your own," he scoffed, "be my guest." Without needing much more ushering, he watched the youths go in teams to their tents, keeping an eye on which marquee one of the older ones amongst them, who had been particularly annoying that day, went to.

Once all were settled he went to his own pitch, some distance from the children, and began preparing what he referred to as a 'building of character'. *A maiden camping trip they'll never forget.*

He waited two and a half hours, patiently, tucked away in his tent, watching the marquees with excitement. *It's gonna be good!* Quietly slipping out of his shelter, he tip toed across the campsite, targeting the structure he knew the most children would be in, *and the biggest shit of the lot.*

With great delicacy he pulled the zipper to the marquee entrance down, and crouching on hands and knees, slid inside. Softly, quietly, he made his way to the back of the tent, being careful not to disturb any sleeping scouts. In position, he readied himself.

"You let me in!" He screeched, rapidly blinking his torch on and off, *"MOTHER?"* He barked, nudging some of the stirring children.

"AAAAAAAARRRRRRR!" A howl filled the tent. Bodies leapt up, scrambling, crying and moaning. They frantically pushed around in the dark, through the flashing light. Tony struggled not to burst.

"WHAT'S HAPPENING?" A young boy squealed. He could see their petrified faces rushing through the marquee with each surge of his torch. The scouts fled together in a wild panic, charging, they tripped over each over, making for the tent's exit, out into the night.

Exploding with laugher, Tony scrambled after them on all fours, chasing until he dropped his torch. With muffled giggles he pushed aside camping equipment, snorting through his nose in stitches. *Brilliant.* He thought. He couldn't stop sniggering. *Best one ever.*

Rummaging back through the equipment for his light, and calming himself for the fading alarm of the youngsters outside, his ears perched at what he thought was a whisper coming from the back of the marquee. Its far end was distorted by complete darkness. He glanced, exhaling a final spell of laughter through his nostrils.

At last he felt the handle of his light, pulling it from beneath a rucksack he pressed the 'on' button. It didn't work. "*Mother?*" A faint voice called from the rear of the tent. Feeling a sudden chill ride his skin, the scout master span about, fixating on the darkest part of the marquee.

A black figure twitched.

He turned to flee. The tent's entrance was shut. The zipper up. He scrambled for it, trying to drag it down yet it wouldn't budge. "Let me out!" He cried, yanking again. "Let me out, you little shits!" Turning back, his torch briefly flickered, revealing two small shadows rapidly approaching before the light died.

"*Mother.*" They whispered.

"*NO!*" He yelled, grasping his chest as a horrific spike of pain stabbed his heart.

In the woods somewhere, far, far from basecamp, a chorus of hysterical screams ruptured the night. Young voices called out. *HELP!... HELP!* But there was no helping them. Not now.

"*What happened?*" They would ask each other, at first.

"*It was an accident.*" Some would say.

"*We didn't touch him.*" Others mumbled.

When questioned why the marquee door was cut open, the investigators bought it had always been cut, because the zipper was jammed. "What reason would the children have to hurt him?" One officer on the scene muttered to his workmate, "it's not like he'd given any of 'em black eyes."

Squeaker

There was a full moon, and I'm *trollied*, talking… *plastered*. I'd just nodded to Jim and he'd give me the tosser sign, so I knew he was alright, then I took a detour through the park because it was cold and I was *sloshed*.

Strolling through, along the main path, don't know what time it was, definitely early hours, pub and clubs are shut. I get to this bit in the middle and there's bunches of trees and bushes and all that, and I'm not gonna lie, my arse started twitching a little bit. Path went from looking like a short cut to my bed, to an endless dark tunnel where every bleak thing imaginable was gonna happen to me.

I just kept looking at the moon, looking up… and forward, sort of… stumbling forward because I'm *rat arsed*. I feel the nausea come on strong. I can still taste the sambuca at the back of my throat and hear nob head Jim shouting *"another one!"* I swallow it down anyway and keep stumbling.

Not sure where abouts it comes from, but I start hearing a faint *whistling*. It ain't in the trees, I can't tell where it's coming from, and I'm not hanging about to find out. My visions getting worse now 'cause I'm… *bit tipsy*.

I started sprinting. Kept hearing the whistling. It weren't getting closer, it weren't getting quieter, and I start tripping out. I'm running, running, running. I can hear my heart beating, I can feel the bit on your neck you touch to check your pulse *pounding* like it's gonna burst.

I dunno how far I ran but the trees all cleared off on one side where the path veered round to the right.

Clear space, and no bloody whistling. I was sweating my arse off. That's when the sambuca came up. Just a little bit into the back of my throat. It made me heave. I rushed over to a park bench and huddled onto it, yacking over the side.

I *BARFED* about 6 times. Bits of chips and kebab, carried on about 6 pints of Sambuca, you *nob*, Jim.

Someone touched me.

"Piss off!" I shouted, spinning about quick. Some little old man jumped back looking as startled as me. "What the hell you doing?" I spat on the floor, ready to get sprinting again, weren't gonna hit an old boy.

"*I saw something in the water.*" He said. His voice was raspy. I quickly checked the treeline. I knew there was a lake past it, it was pitch black though. When I looked back he was glancing about, looking up and down the path.

"What was it?" I asked. His lips started trembling, and I started feeling real uneasy. He shook his head, gazing at the trees himself.

"*A little girl... She said she knew my name.*" He looked up the path again, and I saw the moonlight glint off his eye. *Screw this.* I ran. As fast as I could. Away from the trees. Along the path. There were streetlights up there. *I just RAN.*

He started chasing me. Heard his feet pacing after mine, and it sounded like there was more than just him. Loads of feet pacing after me. I didn't look back. *No no no.* His breaths sounded heavy. Proper heavy. Started sounding like he was *gurgling*, or *grunting*.

I was getting hysterical. I didn't stop running until I was clear of the park. I couldn't breathe barely, just pain and lack of breath. I didn't stop moving. I kept pacing up the first street leaving the park, holding my heart, hoping I'd calm down. I was so freaked out.

Up the empty streets, walking, walking, looking about and listening for anything nearby. The quiet was making me even more paranoid. *Any* far away noise stressed me. Any street I turned down was just empty and silent.

Up by a square near my house where there's a few shops, I took a sit down to catch my breath and calm myself before heading home. I saw a ripped newspaper with yesterday's date on it. It said a child's body was found in the park I'd just walked through, and the suspect was still on the run. A strange detail caught my attention on the report, '*she looks like she's been mauled by a wild animal.*'

I got my phone out. The screen was blurry. Loads of missed calls from Jim.

Trying to focus, and phlegming out the last of the sambuca sick from my mouth, I dialled his number. It must've rang about fifteen times, every one went through to his answerphone. "*Call me back and I might call you back.*" What does that even mean?

He never did pick up.

Hustle

Those scripts went down a storm. I was offered a pretty penny for publishing rights and cut myself a half decent deal on royalties for when they hit the T.V screen. I really couldn't believe it, if I'm honest, I mean, I knew I had some half decent ideas in my head and in my books, but for it to *really* happen… well… what can I say? I was over the moon, so to speak.

On the afternoon I went to sign those deal papers with my agent, we were invited to a *big*… well, I say big… we were invited to a party in the heart of London. Some cat in the industry was made aware of my name, apparently they kept a keen eye on who was coming up, and whoever it was, from other whispers I heard over the years, they'd keep a sinister eye on, sort of thing, making sure we were writing within the accepted *agenda* or so, so I heard, was never a big one for politics, just liked to write, you see.

Anyway, this party was smashing, *grand*, the place had red carpets, big dangling chandeliers and one of those two side spiralling staircases, like royalty it was, I'd never seen the likes of it. I didn't recognise too many faces 'cause I was new to the industry, but apparently a lot of them knew who I was, and that was nice. Lots of congratulations that night, *lots* of them!

Amongst the whole lot, I got talking to this one particular brunette, and she was a *real* brunette, not like the last one, 'ey? Well, we got chatting. She was a beautiful woman, curvy and pretty, and made me laugh, too. I was half expecting her to tell me she had to go at any second and get back to her husband, but no, not this one.

All night we spoke, had a good chuckle, even had a dance with her once the Dutch-courage was high enough. I told her about mum, too, about how she wanted to be up in the lights when she was a young'un, she liked that, said talent must've ran in the family. I didn't tell her about the other stuff, though, not then, anyway.

She was a marketer and was trying to build her profile up. The thought of working with her was exciting for more reasons than one, let me tell you! She seemed keen to offer her services, so before I left the party I arranged a dinner date with her, that way I could play it cool if I was getting the wrong idea and she was only interested in business, and not seeing if we might go anywhere.

The date went good. *Really* good. I remember seeing her to the taxi, and I gave her a peck on the cheek, then she give me a peck on the lips and said goodbye! When I got back to my one bed flat, I sat down, and really just felt inside like something good was about to start in my life.

After all those years of what I look back on now, and just consider a waste, those warehouse years I wouldn't go back to if it meant another 90 years of life. I'd never go back to them, *never*, but that night, when I sat down on my sofa, I understood then, I had to go through them all to get where I was. Those years moulded me, they'd made me who I was in that very moment, and *that* was gonna be the start.

I knew what I was going to do, and I knew who I wanted to hold on to now. I really had what it took to get somewhere, my agent and this girl made me *truly* believe it. All I needed to do was *write*.

Maternity

I'd been dropping subtle hints all day. "You're going to love it this evening." I hoped she was as excited as me. It was getting on in the afternoon and I could barely contain myself.

I'd been planning the proposal for months. The moment we decided to come to New York in fact. The perfect place. The perfect time. There was a little restaurant near our hotel, nothing fancy, just as much as I could afford. That was going to be the place.

During the day, though, she caught my attention. We were stood on the crown of the statue of liberty. "I've got something to tell you." She said, smiling at me.

"What is it?" I asked. She just reached up and kissed me.

"I'll tell you tonight." I smiled back as she turned away. The sunlight tickled off her silhouette, highlighting her face with a line of gold. *She's beautiful.* I put my arm around her and we stared out across the water at New York. The city line was stunning. I squeezed my wife to be against me, embracing the breath taking view.

On our way down we decided to pass through a local cemetery. A silly thing we enjoyed doing, to see how far back the dates went. The first one we came across looked amazing, the architecture was capturing.

Passing through some ancient looking gates, we began circling the plots, and as our attentions on the stones grew, we pointed out numerous names of people from as early as the thirteen-hundreds. Straying from my partner, my attention was drawn to a lone plot.

In the clearing a single grave stood. A small, insignificant piece of granite giving a brief description of a female who died, just thirty-eight years of age. It said on the stone, '*defeated cancer*', and for some time I stood, wondering, what it was that could have possibly beaten *her*.

Ledges

She said yes, and she was pregnant. When we got back home my agent helped us get moved into a little house just outside the city centre. When you're in the know with the right kind of folks, and getting them some earnings, they're keen to help, and I was very grateful at the time, _very_ grateful.

We had a little daughter, birth went fine, few months later we got married. Mum came up to see the vows, and one of my brothers, my agent and his family too, rest were my missus' family, but that was alright. It was nice. It was only a little do.

Weren't long after all those happy moments that my mum passed away… It'd been a spree of such good news, and it all came crashing to an end. She'd been in and out of hospital by then, all sorts of aches and pains she'd say, all sorts. Still not quite sure now what it was that finally got her.

We did the funeral, both brothers and sisters and their families turned up, which was nice in a melancholy sense. It was good to see them all, really, can't see any of them now, guess it's what comes with being the youngest of the lot. You live a bit longer, but you live with a lot less, especially in these later years.

Anyway, between all the madness, thanks to my wife's hard work, I'd been asked to send off some screenplay concepts for a new T.V programme. It was going to feature half-hour 'mystery' scenarios. I was overjoyed. Felt like my childhood fantasies were becoming a reality, _I_ was gonna get to write the shows I used to watch as a young'un. _Incredible_ I thought, it really was incredible, for me at least.

I got to work straight away, got my little black book out, and got to writing the best I could come up with.

Fireworks

It was bonfire night, I think, the 5th of November, or is that fireworks night?

We set up the rockets in a long line, right down the yard. I don't remember who ignited them. All at once they were sparking up, flaring, and then the panic began.

They *all* tipped over. We RAN. Jumping and hiding behind anything we could whilst these fireworks flashed bright across the garden. The garage at the end lit up, and the rockets sprang towards us exploding *everywhere*.

People were shouting out, fearful, screaming, then all at once it was over. We laughed. A child might have been crying. When we stood back up the night sky turned white… The entire sky, from pitch black, to a searing luminous *white*. I remember lifting my hands to shade my eyes from the sheer potency.

A fireball appeared amidst the stars. It looked small at first, yet it rapidly grew, to the diameter of the moon then gigantically more. It hurtled through the atmosphere turning *everything* to daylight. The blazing inferno roared across the horizon leaving a thick black smog in its wake. We all stood in awe, staring. Just… *staring*.

Ripping passed us, it disappeared out of view behind our houses, appearing to arch down towards whatever unfortunate population it was about to annihilate. *It's over. A comet of death.*

A moment later the great blazing inferno thundered back into view, breaking the sound barrier at ungodly speeds around the line of the sky. Just as it entered our sights and flew in, so it projected back the other way, burning through the night, unstoppable.

As quickly as it came, it vanished again into space, returning the Earth to darkness. *"What happened?"* I asked. Nobody panicked now, nobody laughed or cried. We stood… silently.

Frittered

"Get up to much on your week off, Mike?"

Crikey, what a question. I volunteer for an archaeological dig-site firm, it's pretty exclusive, well, extremely exclusive. Last Friday afternoon I got a call, they'd found something over in the states, California, and were taking emergency measures to get all available hands over there, flights and board paid, they just needed people there ASAP.

They wouldn't tell me what it was, and said when I arrived in Cali I'd have to sign a waver… *a ruddy waver*, now I was interested. I said I got until Friday and I need to be back home for work. I'd sign the waver if they wanted me for the next six days.

When I touched down at the airport I was escorted to meet up with the rest of the group who'd agreed to sign, most of them dressed like something out of India Jones. I saw two fellas arguing amongst themselves, shouting and swearing, one of them claiming he'd discovered some new species of something, the other said *he* had, then one of them starts swinging, smashes the other bloke's glasses and one ends up with a bleeding nose, all whilst armed airport security rush the group and make us sit against the wall because of these two clowns.

Next thing I know we're all split up and getting put into the backs of big lorries, loaded in like sardines, they shut up the ends and we're off. No windows, no air con, kid you not, it was *boiling* in there, stifling, I was sweating my nads off.

I'd say we were in those for a few hours. Most people were asking what they thought we were heading out for, we came to the conclusion it was a dinosaur site, and it got me excited, I hadn't been on a live dinosaur dig before, to get to work on a fresh one was going to be like Christmas Day.

It wasn't until nightfall our trucks pulled up. I can barely remember staggering off the back, out of the trailer, and just feeling absolutely shattered. Talk about depleted. I was hungry, *stank* of B.O, crikey, I never smelt B.O like it, and felt ready to nod off at any moment. Couldn't keep my eyes open!

I didn't moan for long. This place we pulled up to was stunning. A humongous hotel with light pink roof tiles and beige walls, palm trees everywhere, could smell a swimming pool in the air, and I tell you what, the warm breeze was incredible, it was like something out of James Bond.

The idiots had stopped arguing, the numpties all dressed like Indiana were stripped down, and we were served up some fine dining and top quality wine to boot. Was amazing. I was shown to my room, the bed was the biggest most comfortable mattress I've ever laid on. My head must've touched the pillow and I was out like a light.

Next thing I know, there's some manic screaming in my ear, and I mean *screeching* like you wouldn't believe, and I kid you not, I hear a *ROAR*, like an animal's *roar*. Now I'm thinking maybe it's not a dinosaur dig site. They've actually found something *live*. It's going to be like Jurassic Park!

I rushed out my room, didn't even put a top on, abs and pecs out, straight down the corridors, out of the complex, perfect blue sky, rushed to the pool and an almighty *SPLASH* surges up and a god damned *BEAR* bursts out of the water, starts thrashing about everywhere and the screaming ensues.

Not a clue what I was doing running out towards the sound of danger, I'm thinking stupidity, you're probably thinking bravery. This beast suddenly focused on some poor girl and it charged her… I froze. I thought it was going to kill her. She broke down in tears on the spot. Didn't try to run, just collapsed and huddled up into a ball.

"Stop!" I shouted. The bear slobbered and growled, grunting, gnashing, showing its teeth and flashing its claws, it rushed right over to her and just as it raised its gigantic arm to swipe, some little tiny dart appeared right on its snozzer!

My goodness, this thing recoiled, did a 360 trying to get the dart out of its nose but it couldn't! Next thing you know it was asleep! Massive grizzly bear, asleep in this hotel pool area. *It was humongous.* I didn't even know grizzlies lived in Cali, come to think of it, I'm still sure they don't. The poor girl just laid there and kept crying. I can't blame her either.

Some fellas I saw driving the trucks came and took her away, and that was the end of that. Everyone was just pretending like it never happened, it was mental.

Next, we're all being lined up to sign our wavers. No questions, no answers. We're loaded back into the trucks and on we go. Second trip was about an hour. Before we even got out I knew we were at least at the sea. I could smell the salt and hear the waves. I was getting excited again, and a little worried as well. Not a big fan of being out on the water.

Soon as we stepped back off those trucks I was just stricken in awe. The view… The *view* of this seaside cove was like nothing you've ever seen. A big 'U' shape of clear turquoise water washing up against a golden sandy beach. Just off-shore there was a build up of steep rockfaces, and they eventually led off, joining onto sharper and bigger edifices going up the coast.

All along this enclosed strip, must've been private because there weren't a single soul on it, were these abandoned huts. They looked pretty old, made with wood and palm leaves, probably ancient in fact, and they were tiny, it'll sound mad, but it looked like some kind of pigmy village, all the little houses were on bamboo stilts, all looking out onto the water.

There were a load of rubber dingy boats lined up, all with small engines in them, and next we were put on to those. Tell you what, I'll have to take back my claim I'm not a fan of the open water, being underneath that clear blue sky, sun blazing down, it was just magnificent. You've not seen clear water like it, either. Didn't matter how deep the sea got, you could see all the way to the bottom, just beautiful, sand and stones, it was incredible.

The boats took us about 100 foot off shore, then started slowly paddling us in towards the steeper rocky surfaces of the cove, and there, just beneath the waterline, I kid you not, one of the eeriest things I've ever seen, not on T.V, film, not even in a bluey.

Now, if you didn't know, sharks don't have bones. The only thing that completely fossilises are their teeth, and it takes hundreds of thousands of years. 'Why you telling me that?' You're probably thinking, *well*, embedded in this stone surface rested the exposed remains of an *absolute giant*. A completely clean, perfectly preserved cartilage structure.

It was the remains of a megalodon. Picture the biggest great-white you can imagine, then treble it. We're told these things died out hundreds of thousands of years ago. Too long for cartilage to survive in conditions like this, but here it was, *perfectly preserved megalodon cartilage*.

It was literally *embedded* in the cove's ridge, so huge, it was visible through the water from the shoreline once you knew where to look, AND GET THIS, *it had a ten-meter long harpoon lodged in its head*. Somebody was hunting this thing, some ancient marina *actually* killed this monster, and we can carbon date it all.

I spent what time I had on site geared up in diving equipment, and with painstaking steps we started clearing away the ocean sediment, slowly getting to the fragile cartilage. I just couldn't get my head around it, *how in all hell was a megalodon's remains, void of all organic material, laying here, exposed in a shallow sea cove?*

By the time I left we'd just extracted the spear which was literally disintegrating if you touched it too hard, we got it free though, and it was being prepped for a laboratory. The shark's remains themselves were still being exposed. Best of all, and I mean this with all my heart and soul, best of all, I got to keep one of its teeth. The thing is literally bigger than both my clenched fists put together, it's like a dinner plate, kid you not!

But anyway, no-one's gonna believe all that, even I *could* tell them.

"Not too much, mate, just sat around and had a few beers."

Interest

We were living in the city when it all started, right on the main road as you come through off the big blue suspension bridge. I still see mad folks racing down off its slopes on their pedal bikes, riding with no hands… It's crazy. The sea looks bright and serene beneath, and there's always some homeless fellas loitering on the walkway where you get off, too. That's a pain in the backside.

So, probably a few hundred meters past the bridge and water, it's all built up, proper concrete jungle, our city buildings start. Rows of multi-storied houses on the right, and similar on the left, but the ground floors on that side are all shops. About three hundred meters past the bridge, on the right, is my pad. On the left, just across the road, my favourite place to eat.

When I was a kid I thought it was great. You'd go in, and it was just a desk in the corner, and across the sunny hall, lit by big windows looking out onto the main street, there were lots of little circular tables with flimsy looking wooden chairs around them.

You'd order breakfast, and the lady, my mate's mum, would go straight out the door, and within a literal minute she'd come back with your food. *A minute.* One minute, food, on the plate, served.

We followed her once when we got a bit older, and it turns out she was running to an 'all you could eat' buffet up the road, loading her plates, and rushing them back. Not a clue what was going on. Don't know if she paid for it or what.

One day me and the lads were sat in there getting some grub, and just paying up. My mate owed me a bit of cash from the weekend so he paid the bill. I remember the little pad the receipt was in closing, and the *whole* building started shaking. *Really shaking.*

Everyone in the place jumped out their chairs, acting wild. Me and the boys ran out in the street, across the road, into my house. We rushed upstairs to the backrooms looking out towards the ocean, and the strip of water going under the bridge.

One of my mates put the radio on their phone. There were mad reports of an earthquake. "The grounds at the coast are subsiding, please evacuate your homes." Out in my back garden, leading out towards the water, was the *biggest* industrial yellow digger. Easily as big as my house.

There was a government digger IN my garden. It was shovelling the end of my lawn like it was nothing. Shovelling it away, crane going just yeeting that turf away. "Please evacuate your homes." The radio said. There were diggers all the way up the back gardens, digging away. My entire house was vibrating.

"The government is sending emergency services to prevent the subsidence." The radio spat. But they were already there. When we got there, *they were already there.*

They must've known something was up. But who could predict that? That an earthquake was going to start subsiding the land along the waterfront? The more I think about it, the more it looked like those diggers were causing the disturbance.

Plateau

Thankfully, those concepts were well received. My agent was getting a good amount of interest coming through, too, I really felt like things were going great.

I'd been working on my main body of work throughout that time. '*Between the Mares*', had a lot of horror stories written up, ready to be converted onto the T.V screen, and I really wanted to pursue getting them out there. My agent came to me one afternoon with a different idea though, and, well... 'cause of the money offered, I couldn't resist.

A big production company was after a film script, a full-length movie. I'd never written one but my agent said it'd be no problem for me, I was on fire, and nothing I wrote would be looked at in a negative light.

Me and the missus had just had our second child as well, a lad, perfect little family we were, and she had every faith in me, she doubled down on my own thoughts, that, with the money we could get a really nice place for the kids to grow up in, and for us to live out our latter years.

So, I put the horror writing on the back burner and knuckled down. When I agreed to the project I got a very tidy sum up front, and I must admit, at the time, I believed I'd made the right choice.

I had a successful screenplay portfolio, a beautiful family, and was going up in the world. What was there for me to be upset or worried about? Only thing I remember thinking negative back then, was, I wished mum had been there to see it all.

Greener

Pattering rainfall drummed across the stale leaf roof of a masterfully crafted bamboo longhouse, its foundations embedded amidst the dense thickets of a vibrant rainforest. All about and within the structure's handcrafted walls, a hundred or more dark skinned, tattooed individuals corralled around two chieftains.

Daylight was rapidly fading. There was a dire urgency in the aged males' voices, however they kept their tones down to a light whisper.

"My tribe has seen first-hand what comes through the trees." A minute puncture hole in Omak's abdomen still oozed blood. The leader of the Turah was at his host's mercy.

"Why should we believe your stories?" An angered voice called quietly through the gathering, only to be stemmed by the second chieftain, Zau. He had never seen such dread riding a people as when Omak and his kin rush onto their knees before him.

"You have all seen the skies raining fire, and the *boom* of those things wreaking havoc through the jungle. When the smoke reached our huts, me and my son, and all of us who escaped, we saw, it was the *devil* who rode it."

"The demons of *Tabba*, no doubt!" A dismissive scoff was joined by troubled mutters.

"*Shhh!*" Zau raised his hand, attempting to calm the riled crowd. "Let our guests speak," he whispered, commanding his own tribe with an easy authority.

"When our home was ambushed by those… *demons*… we attempted to flee through the jungle, there was no way we could make it up the cliffs, not with what is left of us. We circled as far as we could, but the fires burn everywhere. All throughout the valley. Our only option, if we are to escape from this… this *thing*… *is* to scale the cliffs, and reach the other side. Zau, yours was the only village left, and we need you."

"Nobody can scale the cliffs."

"My son," Omak lifted a trembling arm, pointing to his longhaired offspring, "he climbed with our gatherers, they are all dead, bar him. He can get us out, but we must hurry." A thunderous crash shook the land. The longhouse juddered with creaking wood, and those inside sprang about.

"Why do you need our help if your boy can take you?" Another yelled through the panic.

"Look about us. We are mostly frail and young, and none of us experienced in climbing. We need your help, to carry what is left of my tribe with you, in exchange my son will lead us up and away from this danger, to better pastures, it is our only hope of escape!" Omak's aged gaze rested firmly on Zau's. "Will you have us?"

Zau nodded, extending his arm to a male he once opposed. They clasped, and under the moon of that night, together, the tribes gathered what food stocks and valuables they could carry, setting out.

Imak, the Turah chieftain's son, led them. Many warriors of the Noa were first unwelcoming of him, however, there was little they could dispute about their situation.

In their wake, the jungle burned. Smouldering boulders of infernal terror rode the skies, horns of some unimaginable threat bellowed through the trees, tracing their every movement. All of them were helpless but to listen to their territories crumbling beneath whatever evil pursued.

Though the base of their ascent was deep jungle, the tribes had known the surroundings all their lives. They grew up in them, hunted in them, warred against one another, and now, in the face of an enemy unforeseen even by their shamans, were forced to stand united in attempts to escape together.

They trekked nonstop each night, letting up only for the elderly to rest their bones. Any who struggled were helped by their company, regardless of which tribe they came from, there was no time for quarrelling, not anymore.

The higher they climbed, the worse the slopes grew. It did not take long for the familiarity of their jungle to fade away, replaced by rocky edifices and open grounds, leaving them exposed between stretches of trees.

On the fourth night, the tribes stumbled to a unified halt. A vocal alarm spread amongst them, calling out for Imak. The young hunter rushed to the summoning, stumbling at sight of his father laying limp, his hand still holding the wound on his punctured side.

"*Pappy?*" He shouted, skidding into the undergrowth on his knees. He grasped his dad's spare arm. "Pappy!"

"I feel light, my boy." His gaunt face was colourless.

"Hold on, Pappy, just a few more days and we'll be out of the valley, we'll be safe." The weathered chieftain released a flurry of coughs, his eyes rolled in his sockets as he tried to keep focus.

"I'm an old man." He wheezed, "and I feel..." His head dipped and he coughed again, the pressure pushing more fluids from his wound.

"Hold on tight, Pappy." Imak pressed his father's other hand to the damaged skin. The old warrior exhaled heavily, his every breath scraping his throat.

"You're a good boy." Imak squeezed his eyes shut. "Help these people, *my son*, take them to safety."

"Help me carry him!" The young male shouted, blinking heavily. "Please."

"You need to lead us, Imak, I will carry your father."

"Thankyou." He said, shaking his aider's hand, bowing with sincerity at his offer.

Despite their efforts, Omak did not last the day. They rested that night, watching fires push across the jungle, billowing pillars of ash into the sky. The horrendous smoke, generated from burning leaves, poured through the branches, chasing those fleeing far up the valley's cliffs.

"What did you see when this *thing* reached your village, Imak?"

"Death. The smoke... and *death*."

"Were there men amongst them?" Imak fell quiet. The twig he rolled in his fingers snapped and he threw it.

"I don't know. They stood like men, but fire came from their bodies... from their *souls*... No. They could not have been men." In the darkness, another scorching ball twisted across what was left of the jungle's once beautiful canopies, and with it, a chorus of horns. The tribes leapt to their feet.

"They are coming for us!" Someone called.

"Gather yourselves! Keep close and stay quiet! We must move on in the dark." With the group mobilising, Imak rushed to his father's lifeless body. He dropped to his knees beside him, and with a stammer, pressed a kiss to his forehead. With nothing left to offer, he returned to his peoples' lead, and together they pushed on into the night.

A gripping atmosphere of paranoia held them. Many bickered amongst themselves, selfishly pushing to the group's head, abandoning whatever team efforts had gotten them this far, enough however held true to the dead chieftain's pact.

Reaching the first rocky outcrops of their ascent, Imak selected some sturdy individuals and explained his people's system of cliff scaling. He was familiar with the surfaces and would climb free hand, embedding pegs and rope tethers on his route. Once enough were lodged, and he reached a safe plateau on which he could cast a safety rope for his followers to secure themselves, his chosen group would follow him, linking the tethers as they climbed, producing a ladder by which the rest could scale the edifice.

With an enveloping smoke billowing from the jungle, fogging their vision, and the commotion encroaching at their backs, the terrified group set to work. Their first tries were clumsy, rushed by the enclosing calls of whatever was burning their lands. *"How much further?"* Many struggling voices would cry upon being pulled to safety over the ridge.

"At least two more full days of trekking." Imak could not lie to them.

"Our food runs low, we must make time to hunt." Some peculiar groan down in the valley vibrated the ground beneath their feet. A fresh layer of alarm spread throughout the tribes.

"We have no time!" A frail looking female intervened amongst arguing males. "Once we are clear of the valley, and this… *destruction*… we can gather ourselves, we can feast and drink, and rest." The majority nodded after her.

"There are four more ridges to climb, the last, leading to the peak…" Imak briefly fell quiet. "*Just four more.*" He muttered, looking at the faces he led. They were lost.

"Imak?" Someone called with an air of desperation. They were looking to him now. All of them.

"Let's go. The further rockfaces are worse to climb, but if we keep our ground, they are accessible, the hunters of my tribe have reached them before."

"Have *you?*" A voice asked. Imak ignored the question.

Heading on into the early morning, those who abandoned their loyalties before returned to help the group, carrying each other towards the valley's top.

Each new edifice was scaled with trouble. The climbing ropes and pegs they used slowly dwindled. Not once did the pursuing horns stop. By the time they reached the highest grounds of their valley, every last stretch of jungle could be seen ablaze. Burnt out spheres of magma lay around beneath, scarring the landscape with marks of destruction.

"Our homes, they are gone." A blubbering face blurted.

"Don't focus on that," Imak said, "the last climb is up ahead, and beyond, our new home, away from danger."

The crowd watched in excitement, cheering his final troubled movements and risked lunges to secure a footing at the very peak of the valley. Pulling himself up, he stumbled on his knees, crawling from the crowd's sights.

Imak looked over the cliff's natural parapet towards those lands his struggling tribe sought to make their new home.

He stared for some time, then turned back. His face was frozen. His expression empty. Without ceasing, he cut the safety chord linking his ropes to the group, rushing to kick the upper pegs securing their route up out of the ground.

"*What are you doing?* We'll be stranded here!" A furious male shouted. They watched Imak look on, drearily, out at the steep passes his company had spent days trekking up, and beyond, across their burnt and dying territories.

With the distant echo of their pursuers bawling in their ears, they watched helplessly as the young leader glanced back one last time at whatever pastures now lay beyond their reach, and with a single effort, leapt from the overhanging precipice, tumbling hundreds of metres below, back down into the valley's rocky slopes to certain death.

Grass

That film was regarded as 'one of the biggest flops of the century'. Didn't get a single five-star review off any so-called journalist, no publishing house, not a single name in the industry had anything good to say about it.

I hid in my house for months on end afterwards, even started going to the bottle again, just to get the pain out my stomach. The pain of sheer cringing embarrassment. I'd presented something for the whole world to see, and not a single soul enjoyed it.

It was even worse than the whole world knowing I'd smashed that window as a young'un, and it weren't just family who knew about it, it really *was* the whole world. Every time I saw a poster or headline my stomach wretched.

I hadn't felt like it since my alcohol days. Waking up, and knowing you've *done* or *said* something terrible, something unjustifiable, but you've already done it, *drunk*, you can't unsay it or undo it, it's too late, the damage is done, and you have to sit in your own pity and misery, cringing inside, wondering *who* the hell it was who'd hijacked your body whilst you were on the sauce.

Blimey, I don't miss that feeling I tell you, not one bit, glad I eventually managed to knock liquor on the head and stay away from the stuff, but during those months, after my film was released, I was in a world of self-imposed misery.

I couldn't handle it, so I cooped myself up in the same house the earnings from the movie bought. I felt wrong even being in its walls. It'd been purchased on a failure, with money I didn't deserve.

The phone stopped ringing as well. My agent stopped calling. The same individual who'd talked me into the mess as good as cut ties with me. He didn't want to be associated with a flop, seemed like the entire industry turned its back on me all at once.

For a few years I became a hermit. At first they were terrible, I'd mope around the house, drink myself to sleep most nights, not sure how the missus put up with it, recon she was about done with me after 6 months, she as good as warned me, but it was about that time I started having a real interest in something new.

Our kids were about 4 and 5 by then, and they were developing real likeable personalities. I realised what a great opportunity I had to simply spend time with them. No money worries, not after '*Greener*' flopped, nobody hassling me for work deadlines, not being pestered to go out promoting new shows, just peace and quiet.

So that's what I done, spent time with the young'uns, really got to see them growing, got to play with them, help them with homework, probably some of my best memories those years, it was a little sweet spot, a place between them being grumpy teens and… well… something that resembles a sack of potatoes I suppose.

During those years something else amazing happened. Something that really made me forget about all the misery of my failing career in an industry I once lived to work for and be successful in.

My two kids from the first marriage made contact. I went into town one day to meet with them, it was the first day I'd been off my property in those 3 years, really the first time I'd interacted with someone who weren't my wife and kids.

Brought a tear to my eye to see them grown up. Really, really one of the best feelings I can say I've ever had, to see those two well, and *smart*, good heads on their shoulders they had. It was a turning point for me, for my mental state.

They said they loved my movie, and had seen all the programmes I'd written for T.V. Well, it made me feel great, they really lifted me out of the slump I'd been stuck in. We continued to meet up over the years, too, I really hit it off well with them, and I'm so grateful for it.

It was after that coffee and what they said that got me thinking about trying to make a comeback. I still had another couple of stories left in me. I bit the bullet and made contact with my old agent.

He was pretty short with me, said horror weren't being looked for at the time, said he could do me a favour and pass on any concepts for more stand alone mystery programmes that might be considered, so, what else was there to do? I got to work.

pArrrrty_!_

'Twas, if I recall reclectly... re-collectly... 'ey? Within the *stinkin'* hole we pirates know as 'Stoley's Rest'. If you're familiar with Rike, you should know well of this hovel. We 'ad entered the Caribbean to transport some ingots, and 'ad 'eard of a big *filthy* reward for the capture, dead or alive, o' a mysterious... mystery fish.

'Twas whispered to be a deep sea diver, for 'twas only seen after the likes of a storm great and vicious, likely bringin' the *bastard* up to crest the waves. Strange noises be heard, far off shore, near the ends of the world I don't doubt. Sailors and captains alike speak o' sounds unheard of, 'part from those that did. Before any man could cast gaze the beast be said to 'ave vanished, leavin' only a glimmer o' light in its wake.

T'ad been a rough few days at Stoley's. It still *stinks* worse than Davey's locker, and fouler worse than what is less, if you catch my drift, *you worthless toss*. Let me sip mi ale, and I shall spin ye a tail... a *tale*.

We'd been stuck up in this battered *box* for the very purpose o' waiting out a *ferocious* storm, for 'twas in this exact time, just after the tempest be gone, we were told the mega fish would expose itself, this mighty *thing* o' the deeps, that many a sailor 'ad claimed to see.

Avast, once the brunt was over, we set sail out of the East due North, and West beyond the South, if ye know these waters ye shall know what I speak of... Let me sip.

We sailed out beneath many a moon, I scarcely recall the suns for I be on mi back when mi crew be scrubbin' and dubbin'. Durin' mi wakin' hours many a crew mate would speak whispers of a shoutin' nature, o' the monster we plunged forth to see with our own blind sights, ya dig?

We 'ad misjudged the storm's potency on our route out to the shallow deeps. Many a night o' terror constricted the crew as thunder and fury, and lashin's o' waves the likes of savage whips against open wounds rattled our vessel... 'Twas with some troubled spirits we made through the brunt of it, giving it our all to overcome the foulest of even odds Davey could send.

Be time we 'ad overcome the untameable wrath of nature, cresting tides of a thousand leagues in height, and oceans of a breadth of several oceans... *and more...* we finally reached our destination. No matter where ye' looked from the crow's nest, 'twas not a man in sight, part from mi crew, and all those ships that 'ad survived the weathering... We 'ad a few come with us, if ye recall me mentioning.

By untold chances, the beast appeared! 'twas lifeless, 'twas motionless on the ocean surface, a great, big, gigantic, humongous scaly silverly fish, and that's when I was 'bout to order the crew to prepare the harpoons. "Avast!" I yelled, from atop the crow's nest. "Prepare the 'poons!" I yelled, I did.

Before we started to stop, one captain, from another ship, boarded mi vessel via plank, 'e approached 'pon deck ordering me to turn the fleet about. "Ye shall not be takin' mi crew down to the locker with ye!" 'e bellowed in mi face, the *shitter*. I didn't want no conflict, but should it've been, 'e woulda been keelhauled beneath mi toes.

I punched the air near him, a warning punch, and where mi fist ceased, so a rip o' thunder clapped the spot. 'e knew it there and then, that should we 'ave parlayed, if I 'ad hit 'im, 'is head off would've come off... *twice.*

Anyway! 'Twas not until we speared it that the beast began to *flash*, just as those stinking pesky liars said it would. It burst with a bright and charming flurry o' potent and splendid colours the likes of which I'd seen before, but not so. They were dazzlin', *strobing*, and luminous, blinding, but *beautiful.*

They broke the cloudy early morning sky, like spotlights against the grey and blue, with reds and yellows, pinks and purples and oranges and greens, all along the horizon, out across the world's oceans I'm sure, so bright they were.

'Twas a most staggering display, and the lights did strobe, mi hearty began to strum a tune aboard deck 'pon is 'monica, another picked up the pipes and a third the strings. Fires were lit and cheers of mirth 'n' joy spread amongst mi crew! Whilst we lanced and eviscerated the beast, purely to get the *bastard* to flash those gorgeous colours, we danced the hup 'n' jig.

I cracked open the rum, the barrels of ale were emptied amongst us and we began to party! The first of its kind it must've been, and likely the last! Into the night, *pissed* as farts, we raved to the blasting thudding music and strobing light show, all whilst the monster squirmed and rived.

Garbage

I was carrying my girl, my Mariana, my sexy Mexicana. She was bleeding bad, and the sirens were still ringing. I'm not sure how close they'd come to hitting us. We JUST managed to scrape down a side ally.

"You okay, Mariana?" I asked, pulling her weight over my shoulder, dragging her with all I had left down this narrow ally. The way was slippery. I nearly lost my footing a few times. Half way down was a big green dumpster, and I made for it. Rushing behind, I let my baby down against the wall and slid with her.

"Why we stopping?" She mumbled, I could hear the attitude in her voice, that fiery Latina attitude. *BANG!* The bin POPPED! Something big in the bin started thrashing around, going crazy! I nearly jumped out of my wits. I moved to my girl and covered her, closing my eyes, waiting to die. The struggling stopped though, then I heard it.

A muffled *whistle,* then a *click,* and quickly a *click click click*, a whistle and a *click* and a BANG BANG BANG! I flinched again at the noise, jumping to my feet. The bin *whistled* and *clicked* again, BANGING and BANGING. With a shaking body I shuffled to the dumpster, leering over its edge.

BANG! I recoiled, rushing back down beside my lady. "It's a dolphin." I said. It was a dolphin in the bin, really bloody, more than my girl, I saw its dorsal fin was missing. *BANG!* I flinched again. I could hear it. I could *smell* it.

"What do you mean?" Mariana asked.

"It's a dolphin in the dumpster! There's a dolphin... IN THE DUMPSTER." Mariana looked hazy.

79

"We're a thousand miles from sea." We really were. It clicked a few more times, *whistling* and *clicking*, *squealing*, as if it was trying to use its sonar, like it was crying out for help.

"I'm telling you, my love, there's a dolphin in there." I stared at the side of the bin.

"Don't be stupid!" She snapped, grasping my balaclava covered face in her soft, sweet hands. "My love, you try to distract me." She looked down at the blood seeping through her top. "We need to get to The Avenue to meet our getaway driver," her head slunk and I reached forward to support her.

"Come on, my love, we can make it." I helped her to her feet. Supporting her weight again, and we went on. It was some distance to the getaway car, and we'd done some *bad, bad* things. I took one last look at the dumpster before carrying my darling on towards our riches.

Time

Well, they didn't get a look in, and I had nothing left in the tank. My little black books were full of horror, yet the only real horror was how my career was turning out. I really wished I'd never agreed to writing a film script... I didn't have the skill set, was just going on what the yes-men around me were saying.

I was 48 by then, still bald, few more wrinkles, kids were as good as grown, still, they'd always be kids to me, all four of them. It was a tough one to swallow, but I knew by then I was old-hat, a has-been. Out of touch with what was currently popular in the industry.

It's strange, I always used to wonder, how could a musical artist write a one hit wonder in their youth, or maybe a string of hits, then twenty years later they're producing trash? It's the same person, do so many of us only have one good idea in our lifetimes? Why can't we just keep hitting the sweet spot with our work?

It's something I've thought about for years, especially since all I do these days is sit between these four walls, and it's about right, I don't think I could come up with a story on the spot like I used to.

Back in the day I could be sitting there, an idea would flash in my head, and I'd write a story, or I'd wake up from a nightmare with the images fresh in my mind, and an hour later have a great little horror put together.

I don't know... maybe it's just me, maybe it's the same for everyone, maybe we're only meant to be 'on form' for so much of our lives, then it's time to sit back whilst the next generation comes along. Who knows.

I must've been out of the game for years by the time I heard from another name in the industry. *Years.* Lord knows how many I lost, and when I stopped dreaming, well, I couldn't even fill up a black book, not with new ideas, sometimes I wonder, *now*, if I remember any new ideas I have… maybe I filled up my memory bit, can't really remember much at all these days.

Ten odd years I went without work, had a couple of bleak ones when the kids moved out, couple of years I was alone then, they'd bring the grand kids around to see me and their grand mum, we didn't sleep in the same bed by then, and I didn't get out much either. Did a lot of sitting around if I'm honest, in my green turner, maybe too much.

One day the missus brought me a letter that'd come through the door. She sat with me whilst I read it. Someone was trying to do a T.V reboot of an early horror series, and they wanted to kick the premiere off with a few written by some names from way back.

They asked if I'd be interested in sending a couple of concepts over, and well, I really liked the idea. It invigorated me, the missus was happy for me, too, it'd been a while since we'd had something new to talk about.

Only problem was, no matter where I looked, I couldn't find my little black books. My little black books full of my nightmares, they were gone, or so I thought, I really accepted at that point I'd lost them.

All my nightmares, *gone*, and I couldn't barely remember what I'd written in them. I still had a few select memories of some of the older ones, back when my mind was good and the dreams were terrifying, and I had a few ideas thrown at me by the family, and with that, I got to it.

Cobblers

The fog had been thick for weeks. Humid and sticky, day and night. It rolled around every year, at the same time, October, clogging the side streets of York with an eerie mist.

Chas stumbled backwards out of the Atlas, caught a cobble and buckled onto extended arms. His white shirt and finely pressed trousers were already basked in various drinks and smeared dirt.

"Think you've 'ad enough, boy." A blurred, towering figure said. The distorted image shut the tavern's back doors. He'd never been out the backway before. A ghostly street became whole. Lined out images of rafters and windows riding high walls above all slammed shut, and a barren cobbled pathway grew prominent to the east and west.

His whirling vision pushed the narrow walkway long and slender on both sides. Grey and dark blue, their stones must've been laid early, since the Victorian era. With a nauseous exhale, Chas pushed his hands to rise but crumbled over himself, retching where he stalled.

A clicking clatter clouded his clarity.

Chas collapsed on his elbows, wincing at the peculiar sounds ringing in his ears. He heaved through his guts until he burst, spouting projectile vomit through his throat, basing the streetway with half digested lumps and fluids. Again and again, heaving his guts up, spraying the floor with bile and innards.

"*Aargh!*" He winced at the wrack, blowing chunks, chundering, he gave up his strength, plunging into his frame, laying wasted against the cold cobbles.

"*Bugger me.*" He spat. He couldn't even remember getting to the Atlas or why he'd been kicked out.

Another clamour clicked in his ears.

Left cheek pressed to the chilly stone, through the haze and swirling horizon, he saw a silhouette appear. A fierce *neigh* blasted into the enclosed street, echoing through the narrow pass, spouting a cloud of hot air into the night. Rhythmic *clips* and *clops* of cantering hooves *cluttered* his thoughts.

"*What...*" Chas whispered, sprawling out on his back to get a look up the road. "*What on earth is that?*" He dribbled, pulling himself onto hands and knees, unable to get a clear focus through his drunken vision. Several identical dark outlines swirled back and forth, struggling to meet.

"Who's there?" The young man shouted, pushing himself onto his feet, colliding with the Atlas' bricks.

"Step back into the gutter, peasant!" A deep northern voice thundered. "This is his majesty's business!"

"*Peasant?*" Chas barked. "Who you calling *peasant*... peasant?" A congregation of three gigantic horses, followed by another two and a drawn cart *clambered* to a *clouting* halt. Chas' vision was stirring before him. He could just make out some feathered tri-cornered hats and funny looking suede outfits.

What? He knew Halloween was close, though was sure it was still a few weeks away. "What's... what's this?" He slurred his words, struggling to maintain a flat footing.

"*HELP!*" A voice shrieked from the wooden carriage behind the wall of towering horses. A banging from inside disturbed the mist, wafting it in the thick street air.

"What's going on here?" Chas yelled at the riders, his confidence held together by booze.

"Stand aside, peasant!" The middle shade with the largest feather shouted. "This is your final warning!" With his orders, the cart banged again. Its decorative doors burst open.

"*Help me!*" A petite figure rushed from between the mares, dressed in a white bonnet, tied about her chin, and an ankle length royal-blue roach layered dress. She waved white-gloved hands at Chas, making her way with a troubled rush out from the corralled steeds.

She grabbed his hands. "*Please.*" He looked down at her, at the outline of her chin and slender nose. Her curled blonde locks captured a beauty the likes of which he'd never seen.

Still feeling the alcohol coming along strong, and with sight fazing into shadowed voids, Chas' ears twinged at what he was sure was some harmonically playing pipes and strings, faintly, carrying through the night. He tried to refocus his senses.

"Step away from his majesty's prisoner!" The same authoritative voice boomed.

"*His* majesty? We got a queen, dick 'ed!"

"Blocking orders of his majesty is treason!" The towering shadow leapt down from his mount's saddle, landing on the blue cobbles beneath without the faintest *wisp* of a sound. "Step aside or pay the price!"

Chas' view was getting blurrier. He could barely even make out the figure's body. It looked like he could

see straight through him. "*Don't let him take me again.*"
The lady whimpered, pulling herself close.

"Somebody hand him a blade! I will not kill an unarmed man!"

"*Here.*" The young woman whispered, pulling a sword from the rolls of her dress, keeping it hidden from her imprisoners. "When he turns away, you must strike for the neck."

"*What?*" Chas whispered back, looking down at the lady's endearing face.

"*You must.*" She wrapped his hand around the blade's handle.

"This is your final chance, peasant!" The overbearing male approached Chas. *It's got to be a joke.* He thought to himself. *It's gotta be Halloween.* "Somebody, throw this man a sword!" He turned to look at his peers. The blue dressed lady stepped aside, and without a serious thought, Chas swung the weapon she gave him, just as she told him to. "HATH AT -"

The strike stunted his target's yell. It sliced his neck cleanly. Chas was sure he felt it grate through. Blood sprayed violently from the beheaded body, spouting like a fountain all over the backstreet, joining his sick, spreading into streams along the alley's cobbles.

"*Oh! Thankyou!*" The beautiful girl sprang back into his arms. She grasped his face, but he couldn't feel her touch. "He was escorting me to the gallows." She jutted forward, kissing his lips. "This is the third time… Won't *you* take me to the show?"

"*What?*" Chas stumbled backwards, shocked at the raining blood all about him. He released the weapon handle he clutched. Nothing fell to the floor. With his mind and vision still spinning, the young man turned and ran.

Not far down the street he found his way back up the side of the Atlas, onto the main road. He saw blue flashing lights. "HELP!" He called. "Help me!" Waving his arms, he corralled a police car to him. "Help!" He cried again.

A uniformed officer rushed from the vehicle. "What's the matter, son?" They asked, looking as confused as Chas did intoxicated.

"I…" The young man started blubbering, he fell to his knees, ready to throw up again. "I think I just killed someone." He cried into his hands.

"*What?* Where's the incident happened?" Chas pointed daintily towards the Atlas.

"On the cobbled street behind the pub." The officer looked up, raising an eyebrow.

"You tryina' 'ave me on, son? There's only fields behind the Atlas, last building on the lane."

"*What?*" Chas said himself, trying to focus his sights. He was too wasted.

"How much you 'ad, mate? You know 'alloweens still a few weeks away, don't you?"

"I swear… There was a horse and cart, and a woman in a blue dress… She told me to do it. I swear…" The officer looked at Chas, scrunching their face and exhaling with humour through their nose.

"Alright, sit in the back of the car and I'll 'ave a look." They grabbed Chas' elbow, dragging him to his feet. "Throw up in my car though and there'll be some trouble." They opened the door. "'ere, lean out 'til I'm back, and don't go nowhere." Chas nodded. His mind raced. The more he tried to focus on the Atlas, the more he could make out, there really was only darkness behind it. Fields, just as the officer said.

When they returned, Chas was cautioned for wasting police time. He was driven thirty miles west, back to his parents' house, the following day they were informed he'd been drunk and disorderly by the pub owners, theirs was the last spot of the crawl.

Embarrassed and appalled by his own actions, Chas went back to work. He had some months left of his summer job before returning to his studies down south. He laughed often with his friends and peers over the drunken night. Just another story to tell. Many of his drinking mates who were on the work's pub crawl told him how gone he was.

I must've passed out when I was booted. He eventually concluded, shrugging the experience off as 'just one of them'. Summer work was successful, he made more than enough money to pay for his next semester, and as he began digging through his piles of clothes he would take back to halls, kneeling beside his washing machine, the young man came across the shirt and trousers he'd buried in his clothes bin.

He exhaled with humour, pulling out the dirty white top. He could see the mud where he'd landed on his back when he was removed from the Atlas, *and the beer stains.* There were a lot of beer stains. Chas smiled at the blotches of memory from the night. *What a mad one.*

He chuckled to himself, pulling out the now wrinkled black trousers. Turning them inside out, he went through the side pockets and clawed out some old change. Just before he tossed them into the dryer, he whipped his hand into the back pocket and bucked, releasing the trousers, he collided with the kitchen wall behind. *"What the hell?"* He whispered, staring at the discarded clothing.

Chas' breathing became heavy. He took a moment to gather himself, slowly crawling to the black material. With hesitance, he pushed his hand into the pocket again and grasped whatever soft *thing* was in there. It was a white glove. He held it up, staring in disbelief at the small mitten.

"It can't be." Chas whispered. *HELP ME!* The girl's screeching voice rang freshly in his ears. *Won't you take me to the show?* His head grew dizzy.

"It was real?" He muttered quietly to himself. *"No… someone must've placed it there, someone from the pub, for a joke."* He laughed a little, feeling some relief surge through him. *HELP ME!* Her beautiful face was so vivid in his imagination. *"Just a dream… just a dream."*

He rushed to his computer and looked up silver-laced gauntlets. The one he held was tiny, and dirty, but looked so well embraided, he couldn't imagine anyone at the Atlas wearing a pair of them, nor slipping one in his pocket. *They must have*, he thought. His search results turned up an endless list spanning from modern day to early history.

Next he searched for blue military uniforms and tri-cornered hats. There was nothing relevant. *He's escorting me to the gallows.* He recalled her frantic panics, and searching up the topic, found a long history of public executions dating back from the 1800's.

Chas slumped in his chair. "It can't be… it's just a trick." With his wild ideas in mind, the young man left his parent's house and got in his car. He drove in day light out to the countryside, to the Atlas. He needed to see where he'd fallen, where he saw her beautiful face.

On arrival, he circled the old village pub, tracing its moss laden limestone bricks. *It really does look medieval.* Around the back, the police officer was right, there was nothing but open fields. No cobbled walkways, no enclosed street nor buildings lining it. For a moment he stirred, believing he heard the faintest clattering of hooves in the air, however on focus, it was just the wind whipping across an empty countryside.

He went back home, back to work, to his studies, keeping hold of the tiny white gauntlet. Everywhere he went, he took it with him, and at the end of the year came back to the Atlas, on the same night, and waited for the same time to go outside, behind the pub. Of course, there was nothing to be seen, still, the young man could not let go. He knew what he saw, he knew it was real.

Every year he would return, a frail old man, hobbling on his walking stick, peering out of the back door at the same time, on the same night, *every year*, without fail, desperate in his wonderance of who he'd met that night, and what he might have seen at the show.

Allotment

On a crisp, 80's Christmas morning, shivering with the cold, Hal pedalled his way up an unrelenting hill. His creaky pushbike climbed steadily up the slippery incline, made all the worse by a howling icy wind, nicked with flutters of jagged snowflakes.

In the early hours, the only visible entities were those of looming snowmen, rolled up and stood about along the quiet roads, watching in silence, staring as he pushed onwards towards his only getaway, his beloved allotment.

It would be some time yet before daylight, before he could look clearly at the faces of his family.

He could hear them in his ears, hear the in-law's snidey remarks, '*lazy though, isn't he? Barely ever at work, not proper work, anyway, just sits on his backside.*' Day in day out, hear the nagging, snarky tones, see his wife dressing up in the mirror, hours on end, getting dolled up, '*just nipping out to see the girls*', off out again, not getting back until the early hours, stinking of aftershave, then there was his teenage brat, always grumpy, always moaning, '*why do I have to have YOU as a dad*'.

With a tear in his eye, he reached the site of his plot. Hal released a quiet sigh of relief. *Feels more like home than home.* It warmed the empty voids of his cockles. Parking his bike, he glanced about, then unlocked and entered his shed. He lit a single candle, selected a small bottle of ale, turned the radio on, keeping its tone low, and pulled a hand-gun from his bag.

'When the snowman brings the snow' crackled through the speakers, *always hated that song*. He popped his bottle lid and sat at the table, raising it to his lips, he took one swig. Hal stared blankly at the shed's interior, pointing the revolver at his temple. "Happy Christmas, bastards."

It exploded, ripping his skull to pieces, splattering tissue and bone everywhere.

Sat around the table rested the partially decomposed remains of three others. His wife, mother-in-law, and daughter. All had the same biological defects. Severe head trauma and crushed jugulars. The family sat in peace as the next Christmas song aired. A home away from home, at Hal's beloved allotment.

Reminisce

There was something bitter-sweet about sending those concepts off. It's a little strange writing words from the perspective of old age… never saw it sneaking up on me, but, well, here I am.

I suppose I weren't *that* old when I wrote those, in my 60's, probably, don't remember too well now. When I finally found my little black books again some years later, I felt like… I don't know, like I never really fulfilled my potential in life.

I lost sight somewhere along the way of what I was really after… *my dreams*, my childhood dreams. Sometimes I really wish I could say I'd seen them fulfilled, that I'd seen my collection of horrors up on the T.V screen, my own series, '*Between the Mares*', that I'd be known in the industry for it, just like the ones I used to watch when I was a young'un.

I was trying for it at one point, I really was, I allowed myself to be steered off course, I suppose, and… well… I guess I never really got back to it. All those years I had to get back to it… Everything that's happened between sitting in my parent's house as a little lad, watching those shows and imagining being that person, the one who made them, and *now*, now I'm an old boy. Can't even remember the nightmares anymore… it all seems to have gone in the blink of an eye.

When I look in the mirror, I can still see the man who got me here. He looks a little different… A little worn around the edges, but all the features are still there,

there's still a twinkle in my eye. Always will be. Still, to think I never pursued that road… I never truly gave it all I could've… that'll eat at me until my grave.

It's a shame. I don't think I've got any stories left in me. Not anymore. Not these days. The carers won't even leave the pens with me. They say something happened with them… I don't remember what. Nurses are always coming in and asking me 'don't you remember?', what could I remember that I *don't* remember? I just don't know.

Sometimes I think about writing. I think about having an idea, but… well, I don't have any. And I don't dream no more. I can't even get a story from there, not like I used to when I was a young'un, and I suppose, even if I had achieved them, what difference would it have really made in the grand scheme of things? 'ey?

I wonder if I could've done something more with my life… something *heroic* like, you know? I wrote a few stories here and there, never wrote anything that changed anyone's life, not what I know of. Never produced a script to help anyone out of depression, or PTSD or anything like that, when I think about it, I suppose I never really did anything of worth, not really.

I wonder if, even if you go out your way in life to try and really make a difference, if it matters in the end anyway… Do we get rewarded? When you close your eyes for the last time, for truly making a difference? Or does it make no odds no matter what happens at the end of the day…

Afterlife

Before the war, there was a lad born named Gordon. He arrived into a large, loving family. He was well looked after, and praised often. He saw no troubles come from that which posed such a large threat to his country, for he was very well sheltered.

He made many friends in his youth who he would continue to share good relations with. He was raised a Christian, and held onto his beliefs as he aged with a dear passion. He was enlisted as a medic during the second war, and there he learned a great deal about keeping people alive.

When the conflicts passed, he met the love of his life, and made a wonderful family, through which he enjoyed prosperous and gratifying years of happiness. It was not until his late 80's, after experiencing an unending spree of memorable moments, he suddenly fell ill to some unknown sickness. It caused him no pain, and surrounded by his family, in a hospital bed, he awaited his last moments.

"Do you think I'll go to heaven, sweetheart?" El squeezed her father's hand, sniffing and wiping her cheek.

"Of course you will, dad, you were a doctor, you saved lives." Gordon closed his eyes, resting them whilst his daughter spoke. "You raised a family of good people, and even kept *mum* happy for fifty years." He exhaled a heavy stint of laughter through his nose, nodding in agreement.

"They were great years... the best, all of them... even the hard times." He squeezed her hand back, smiling. With his efforts his eyes sprang open. He convulsed once, then lay flat.

"*Dad?*" El screamed. She jumped up, rushing into the corridor for the rest of her family, or a nurse. *Anyone.*

He was pronounced dead on their return. A huge number of people attended his funeral. Honours were spoken of him. Rivers of tears were shed. At his request, the respected figure was buried without a coffin. Placed in the same plot as his ancestors.

Once all had settled, above the earth, Gordon's name would be mentioned often, for generations his descendants would speak of him, and always with a passed on knowledge that he was a good soul, perhaps even a great one.

Beneath the ground, Gordon's body rapidly decayed, reducing through the rot to the very basic nutrients and minerals that made up the parts of his animated being. Down and down, smaller and smaller his remnants regressed, being extracted back into nature, from which they were first procured.

When his decomposition was complete, the very smallest particles of his remains, minute, invisible to the eye, building blocks of all that exists in the universe, the atoms of what were once him, slipped seamlessly back into the mass of the planet, they dispersed, contributing to an infinity of other biological and nonbiological collections.

An unnoticeable strand of them, by chance, carried their way into a new part of life. An incomprehensibly tiny collection of matter, that would become the smallest part of a single cell, of which would make up, with billions of others, a single sperm.

In its trajectory, against all odds, it made it to the egg, and a new life came to be.

The child was born into a troubled home. Its parents consumed by substances that replaced their emptiness, and in their pursuit to sustain such an existence, they opted to begin selling their child's orifices in exchange for the junk they injected.

No childhood did this young boy know. Pain and suffering was his, not by choice, no, but for reasons he would never understand. Beaten, raped, and starved, starved of *love*, of compassion and encouragement, of all those things that might give a child a future, and a past to look back on with warmth.

After years of unimaginable abuse, when he became too troublesome to contain and prosper from, he was abandoned. A quivering wreck, fearful of any who approached him, like a ditched dog, beaten all its life by unexposed monsters.

He was tossed into a hostel, and bullied relentlessly by those who spurred rumours of his past.

One day, he fought back. All his pent up anger, released on one who may have known just as bleak an existence as his own, but found a perch of power over another unfortunate soul. The ring leader of those bullies he killed was just a child, a savage, terribly warped child.

The young man was incarcerated, then brutalised by the guards for his actions. They weren't interested in listening to his excuses. He was treated like a rodent in a cage, and his mind became twisted, black with rage and void of remorse for those turning memories.

Before his time was up, he sat with another inmate, battered and bruised, absolved of all sensible thought.

"You know they got electric chairs for folks like you down in Florida." The comment drew his ear.

"What you gotta do to get in one of those chairs?" He asked.

"You gotta do bad things. *Real* bad things." He was told.

One day in Florida, it broke on T.V, a spree of random murders had occurred, committed by a male who escaped from his probation officer's monitoring. Shocking stabbings and butchery no Christian soul could possibly be capable of. The horrific deeds made state-wide news. The perpetrator was caught, and the media were quick to rush in for a one-on-one aired interview before execution proceeded.

"Do you think you'll go to hell, Mr. Laud?" The killer was asked.

"Will I *go* to hell?" He squinted briefly at his interviewee. His face fell blank. His mouth appeared to sulk and his left eye twitched. He blinked a few times in a most peculiar manner before his face became stern again. He scowled mockingly at the camera. "There's no such thing."

Hotel

I'd sit in the chair in my day. When I got home from work, another day done. It was a green turner, could watch the T.V when I swivelled it, screen was mounted on a bracket, only a little one though, not like these days. I'd turn it back to my wife and kids when the news finished. Mostly read the paper. See what bleak shit'd happened yesterday. Always yesterday, the news.

Family was always about then, too. The missus, the kids for a while, then the grandkids every now and then. You don't notice the clock ticking by whilst they're around. Certainly not the years. Not sure which ticked by quicker. Clock keeps turning over twelve, the years though, they keep going.

Phone don't ring much these days, even with these mobiles, don't ring like it used to. Less people to be ringing it, I suppose. Few faces are missing these days...

My chair gets used a lot more now though, well made that. Made *proper.*

Did most of what I wanted. Learned to write half decent. Had some good stories to tell the kids. Grandkids didn't much get them, probably too young. They're good though, the grandkids, clever for their age.

The missus? Yeah... she was good. She was really good. Not sure what happened to her... I... I can't remember now... Just what it is, isn't it...

    ...

    ...

    ...

"*Bill?* Who're you talking to?"

<u>End</u>

Notes from the author:

Hi there! I hope you enjoyed the read.

The concept of a 'Flash Opera' came to me whilst I was walking home from the pub and listening to 1970's Rock Operas. These sprawling musical albums tell the story of a character through a number of songs, and often go out on tandems to explore various ideas and notions their writer's might have had.

Within my own short and flash pieces I could see patterns rising, some would have an aged voice telling the story, (which would become Bill), though most are just writing small fables out of a joy to write, whether it be drama, horror, humour or anything else.

Bringing them together clicked once the idea of Bill being a screenwriter dawned on me, and then it was about structuring the overarching story to produce Bill's Flash Opera.

Hopefully the end product was entertaining to read, and thanks very much for sticking around.

I am constantly working on new projects, all of which I hope to bring to audiences in the not so distant future, so keep an eye out for me! And please share this book with anyone you think might take an interest in it.

Cheers again.

Dom.

Notes:

Sample story from 'Sounds of The Guitar Man: *Stargirl*'

Between the Mares

Relax, or at least, *try* to relax. Let your muscles soften, your limbs fall limp. Let your surroundings consume you. Clear your head of those whirring thoughts. Allow every last road to find its conclusion, then, *just leave it*. Leave it all alone, and focus into the void.

There's fractals, colours, geometric patterns. Harmless hallucinations. Phosphenes they call them. Morphing faces and crawling figures, racing and racing, rapidly approaching. Never quite reaching. All harmless, they say.

Some nights I try to focus on my breathing, to clear the images, to see a calm *nothingness* like I used to when I was a child. It never helps. Not anymore. I heard the voice of a girl I once knew. I think she called my name, but nobody answered.

Cascading light basked through the thickening dust of a vast empty hall, from high rectangular windows long strands reached down, highlighting the skeleton of a hominid, clearly not human, sat posed at a grand piano.

Flakes of dead matter as dense as snow collected upon its archetypal bones, ancient and brittle, unmoved for untold eons, the fossil's crowd had left the auditorium long ago, if any were ever there.

Where she rested was quiet. *Calm*, and quiet. Through a fire exit nearby though, some hearty chatter might've easily caught an ear.

"…It was all over Teresa Green, mate, I'm telling you! The pub door burst open, right there, Dan Gleesac walks in with Drew Peanuts, comes over and grabs Paul Meoff! Well, our mates were at the slots, and Phil McCrackin sees what's going on, so he rushes over with Iva Bigun.

I'm there, too, and we pin these fellas up by the collars, then the barmaid, Tess Tickle, she tells us to leave, but why should we? It was these *dicks* causing the trouble.

Anyway, she threatens to call the *cont*stables, so we all head outside, and that's when things got really mad. We'd all had a fair bit of booze and that, and I never meant to do what I done. It just… sort of… *happened*…"

Out there, at the courtyard's centre stood a wondrous looking tree, above, the stars glistened brightly. It must've been the clearest night of the year, the branches looked bare of leaves, so it was probably autumn, or winter, and still the event drew a large crowd.

What was it? I thought. People looked sad. Sick and angry. They were dressed up finely however, suits and dresses, frivolous hats and shiny boots.

Pushing into the crowd, I realised it was a wedding. *What a night for one.* Many were hurriedly exiting, some with tears in their eyes. "Speak now, or forever hold your peace." I heard, forcing my way between barging shoulders.

"He's been cheating on you!" A female behind me screeched. Rushing forward, her warning faded to the sound of a nattering crowd cheerfully chattering away, gazing with delight at the couple stood beneath budding branches.

The closer I got, the more the tree seemed to blossom, and the crowd, they melded, from disgust to smiles. I could see the couple stood at their heart now, a beautiful girl in a flowing dress, and a hunched over figure stood before her.

Its skin was red, though its uniform pristine. I couldn't be sure, but it looked like a pointy tail hung from the back of its blazer. "Do you take this man?" A voice asked, authoritative, and clear. *Powerful* it was.

"I do." The bride said, grinning ear to ear, stood in her chosen gown, her mask, her layer of dreams, of such grand imagination reality could only fall short. She wore sunglasses. An odd choice on such a dark night.

Beneath them, hurtful to the touch, a large bruise surrounded her eye. The left one. What caused it, none present knew, and from her line of sight, looking out onto *He* she felt so dearly for, a searing light burned.

Above her, that most stoic tree blossomed brazenly, its buds alive and leaves fervent. The man she looked at stood with a broad chin and enticing smile. His gaze pearly white, stature tall and strong. Even so, she squinted, not for the pain of her secrets, but for a blazing sun shining out of his arse.

It warped her perception, stunting her vision of the crowds, blinding her of those wilting branches beyond the blare emitting from what she so dearly loved. Her reality was all she could see, devotion was her giving, and it was her, the closest to the tree, who would see the leaves change last.

An almighty tremor shook beneath the church's courtyard and finely mowed lawns. Past its grounds, towering city blocks trembled. People in attendance rushed to leave, and in the mayhem I fled with them.

Walkways lined canals, their murky waters looked over by towering flats and colourful housing, *were we in Amsterdam?* Buildings arched over the setting, and amongst each street, faces screamed, shoving through tight alleys.

Down at the water's edge I noticed a narrow barge. Its tabled interior was enclosed by a glass ceiling. *Romantic*, perhaps, on a different occasion. I sprinted and jumped onboard with a fellow group of fearful individuals.

The boat surged away onto oily waters. From the rippling surface I could see bridges passing above us, see the imposing buildings' lights turning off and on, and the frantic masses of panicked people following.

A derelict brick overpass lay ahead, yet most bizarrely, there was nothing beyond it. *Nothing.* A single slender figure stood at its apex. She looked old. Her face was gaunt. She was tall. *So tall.* Her white hair floated and rolled around an emerald dress, down to her waist, as if she was submerged.

With a magnified focus, and uncontrollable enticement, I noticed her pupils were missing, her eyes were a faint glowing blue. She smiled, a plump-lipped, arousing smile, and mayhem ensued.

Up there, fear turned to violence. An outbreak of fighting washed through the crowd. I heard an explosion. Fires were lit. Men stabbed each other in the streets, howling around the witch who stood still, still smiling, still looking at me, those tantalizing eyes fixating, *hypnotising, driving me to unobtainable arousal.*

To reckless abandon.

A heavy *thud* shook us. Something struck our craft's glass causing a huge *crack* to web across its surface. People leapt from the canal edges, down onto us, trying to escape from madness.

"Get back!" It was no good. A waterfall of bodies poured from the walkways, hundreds of faceless figures, jumping and crashing into our boat, into our only hope of survival.

I was growing nauseous, I needed to get out, to escape, to flee this hell, but I was trapped. A final weight landed on our portside, and in one motion we tipped. Flipped upside down. Everyone tumbled together, crashing into the ceiling. I didn't hear anyone screaming now.

In my last moment I peered up through brown waters to greedily catch a final glimpse of the witch's smile. The glass gave way and water gushed in. It was quick. Terrifyingly quick. I didn't struggle. Didn't splash. Just let the waters wash over me, let them take me, bit by bit, steal my oxygen, my sight, *my life.*

'Die in a dream, die for real!' That's what they say, well, they rarely end with the pre-mature grace of *death.*

Down in the murk, I'm convinced those calming phosphenes are returning. The colourful fractals are back, and I'm in bed, face down, laying in my usual position, only problem is, I don't notice my breathing.

I know what's coming, even in that state. I know it, I can't stop it, and it never gets any less horrific.

An entity holds my wrists and ankles, presses a weight on my back, pushing me into the mattress. I want to get up, break free, open my eyes and breathe, *but it stops me*. I can't move. I'm stuck, I can't talk, I can't SCREAM! It's got me and I'm never escaping, no matter how much I fight it, *I'm gone*. I'll never get up again!

...

My eyes open. I inhale, *deeply*. I'm breathing. I *laugh*. I stare in dismay off my bed, across an empty room. Grey carpets and curtains. White walls. Bland, *boring*. My breaths are heavy and short. At least I can feel them.

Memory of the nightmare is already fading, bar a few strange details I can't quite shake. The paralysis. The witch. That wedding... and something else...

Free, and focusing, I close my eyes again, helplessly forgetting what I just saw. What I just *felt*. I drift, back into the void, hoping this time I can get through without being caught... but, *I've already heard her voice...*

Notes:

Printed in Great Britain
by Amazon

12601589R00068